Frederick James Crowest

Cherubini

Frederick James Crowest

Cherubini

ISBN/EAN: 9783742809780

Manufactured in Europe, USA, Canada, Australia, Japa

Cover: Foto ©Andreas Hilbeck / pixelio.de

Manufactured and distributed by brebook publishing software
(www.brebook.com)

Frederick James Crowest

Cherubini

CHERUBINI

BY

FREDERICK J. CROWEST

AUTHOR OF

"THE GREAT TONE POETS," "PHASES OF MUSICAL ENGLAND,"
"MUSICAL GROUNDWORK," "A BOOK OF MUSICAL ANECDOTE,"
ETC., ETC.

LONDON

SAMPSON LOW, MARSTON, SEARLE & RIVINGTON

Limited

St. Dunstan's House

FETTER LANE, FLEET STREET, E.C.

1890

LONDON:
PRINTED BY GILBERT AND RIVINGTON, LD.,
ST. JOHN'S HOUSE, CLERKENWELL ROAD, E.C.

TO MY FRIEND,

RICHARD WILLIAM BEARD, Esq.,

A LOVER OF THE OPERA AND THEATRE,

I INSCRIBE THIS MONOGRAPH

OF

CHERUBINI.

PREFACE.

THE diffusion of biographical literature is not to be deplored. Books which tell the stories of great careers serve one grand purpose—that of instructing those who read them as to how lives are lived. The resultant is an example which the intelligent reader knows how to accept and apply. Happily this example is, as a rule, one which may be emulated—for seldom does the mean man receive recognition at the biographer's hands.

The distinctive character, deeds, and productions of musicians deserve, I think, to be recorded equally with those of potentates, warriors, and ecclesiastics—for how marked an influence they have exercised in the modern work of amelioration and culture !

No apology, therefore, is needed for this brief monograph of Cherubini. As a man and a musician there is much that is noteworthy in his career.

His independence of character and strong individuality, his steadiness of purpose, his thorough freedom from servility and deceit rendered him an honest citizen. And what nobler creation is there than an honest man ? Further, in spite of long delayed encouragement and of tardy recognition, he pursued an onward and honourable course. Though kept poor and neglected by those who could well have lightened an artist's mundane burden, he neither pandered to wealth nor squandered his art to enable him to sail the easier over the shoals of trivialities which hamper the unrecognized artist at every step. It was long, too, before the *aura popularis* was largely his. Cherubini, nevertheless, proved equal to the severe test. Thus his life and career will always serve as a not unworthy model for every earnest student.

As a composer Cherubini does not rank with Bach, Mozart, Beethoven, or the last of the Titans of music—Mendelssohn. Nevertheless he was a profound musical thinker—quite a master, but one who lacked great faculty, namely, poetry and fancy in his art. His influence upon music consists in the lofty light in which, by precept and example, he always regarded music. He linked the old style art with the new, and he showed how possible it was to preserve the chaste art of the classic Italian period while decorating it with the luxuriance of modern colouring. Above all, he leavened music with his pure and stately influence at a period when it was tending to an excess in ideality and affected romanticism. He had no copyists —which is to be regretted. Many subsequent composers might have aimed at his style with advantage to their own reputations and to the benefit of music at large. Cherubini was a prolific writer, and if he did no more, he set a laudable example in divesting his own contribution to art of all sickly sentimentality.

F. J. C.

YORICK CLUB,
  STRAND, W.C.

CONTENTS.

CHERUBINI.

"THE last and noblest Roman in the purely classical style of Art," as Baillot has styled Cherubini, was born at Florence on the 14th of September, 1760. The register of baptisms at St. John the Baptist Basilica, records the full name as Maria Luigi Carlo Zenobi Salvatore Cherubini—by no means an insignificant designation, and the more noticeable since the father was no other than an accompanist on the harpsichord at the Pergola Theatre; and who sheltered himself in a modest dwelling in not the most fashionable *strada* of the city.

Cherubini as a child was precocious. Before six summers had made play with him, his father had decided upon a musical future for his boy. He himself took Carlo in hand, and this with such good results, that at the age of ten years the little fellow could accompany figured basses, play easy pieces upon the harpsichord, and make a tolerable noise, for a child, upon the violin.

It is related that at about this early age Cherubini had made such progress with the violin that he was able to replace a violinist absent one evening from the Pergola theatre orchestra.

B

The paternal training, however, was soon changed for other more serious under Bartolomeo and Alessandro Felici, and after them Bizzarri, a singing master, and J. Castrucci, an organist. A short period of such tuition, and there came the boyish impulse to compose something. By 1773 a Mass in D—for four voices and instruments—was ready, and this was publicly performed at Florence, greatly to the delight of its young composer. Thus stimulated, the boy kept at work, and the following year brought to light a second Mass;[1] also a Cantata, entitled *La Pubblica Felicità*,[2] performed at a *fête* in honour of the Grand Duke of Tuscany, who afterwards became Leopold II. Other compositions of these juvenile times were another Mass written in the key of C, for four voices, and with full score accompaniment;[3] a setting of the Magnificat; an Oratorio performed in St. Peter's Church, Florence; and several minor works, scarcely of greater value now than as evidence of the earnest fashion in which young Cherubini was working, and of his exceptional power of handling voices and instruments along the subtle channels of theoretical art, even when he was a mere boy.[4]

La Pubblica Felicità brought Cherubini into notice.

[1] In C, for Four Voices, with full score accompaniments, 166 pp. MS.

[2] This Cantata is for several voices, and was first rendered in a side chapel of the *Duomo*.

[3] 143 pp. MS.

[4] Most of Cherubini's juvenile MSS. have become lost. Their composer always concealed them. Halévy, who withdrew them from secrecy, declares them to possess no sign of the genius which afterwards unveiled itself.

The Grand Duke—afterwards Emperor of Germany—
had been pleased with the music, and on making
inquiry as to the composer, had generously decided
to send him to Bologna, in the hope that so promising a musician might have every opportunity
afforded him for cultivating his talent. Accordingly Cherubini went to Bologna. This was in 1778,
and he remained there four years, during which time
he was fortunate enough to secure the training of the
opera and mass composer—Sarti.

An extended tutelage with a master such as was
Sarti could not fail to prove other than highly profitable to the zealous pupil, who, not puffed up with
conceit concerning his acknowledged powers, was
eager to lend himself to the most rigorous training.
This was not always of the most agreeable character.
Cherubini, for instance, was a youth with several
rough corners in his character, and he failed to see
the advantage of working in a dark and conventual
chamber, with only a glimmering light from a lamp
suspended from the ceiling—a stipulation upon which
Sarti insisted, and which he used vehemently to declare was the only proper condition under which any
great, or good, music could be composed! Nor could
Cherubini easily reconcile himself to the practice of
copying the scores of the old composers—a feature of
study upon which Sarti placed great stress. The
evident advantage of this labour, however, would
appear to have manifested itself to Cherubini later on,
since he continued to devote himself to copying,
even when he had won fame as a composer; so much
so, indeed, that at the time of his death, and when

his papers came to be examined, it was found that he had left behind him between three and four thousand folios of such copied music! Further, when he became a master in the Paris *Conservatoire*, he made all his pupils apply themselves to this music-copying. The labour, doubtless, is somewhat of a drudgery, but a more royal road, or any better method for acquiring strength and freedom in dealing with orchestral combination in composition, there is not. To copy a great score; to analyze it; to ask the why and wherefore of every bar before leaving it; to note the various accompaniments to the several voices and chorus; to examine the progressions and blending of the instruments—all constitute an application and study which well repays the labour bestowed. Text-books and works of method are good, but intelligent analysis of the original minds of music—as seen in the great scores—is better; and no doubt many students have, like Cherubini, realized this.

Happily neither the dimmed chamber nor the imperative score-copying tended to weaken the friendly relationship between Sarti and his gifted pupil. Cherubini went on—an obedient and painstaking pupil, full of intelligence and an anxiousness to excel speedily in his art. Sarti ordered him to abandon Leo and Durante for Palestrina, which he did; the master asked for an anthem, and the pupil supplied twenty. Little wonder that he afterwards became an exacting *Conservatoire* head!

It was through the good offices of Sarti that in 1780 Cherubini received a commission to write an opera for the Autumnal Fair at Alessandria della Paglia.

The work was entitled *Il Quinto Fabio* [1] (Opus 48), which proved to be neither a remarkable composition, nor one which was successful. Cherubini was not more fortunate with several other dramatic efforts which he made subsequently. In quick succession he produced *Armida*, in three acts, represented during the Carnival held at Florence in 1782; *Adriano in Siria*,[2] first performed at Leghorn; *Il Messenzio*, written for the Pergola Theatre at Florence; *Lo Sposo di tre Femine*, *Marito di Nessuna*, played at Venice in 1783; *L'Idalide* and *L'Alessandro nell' Indie*, composed in 1784. Not one of these operas brought Cherubini either money or reputation—in fact they successively convinced their hearers that Cherubini was not to their taste. He was too learned, too solid and emphatic for a populace in quest of exotic and luxuriant melody. The Florentines liked Cherubini in name and feature, but unfortunately they could not be prevailed upon to listen to his music. Thus Clément tells us that Cherubini's countrymen styled him *Il Cherubino*—not for the angelic beauty of his song, but for the charm of his person, his handsome face and beautiful curling hair.

Thus—as in the case of the prophet—in his own land, and among his own people, Cherubini stood in no great favour. It was for a foreign country to adopt and honour him, and for another people to accept him and his music. This nation was the French, who allowed themselves and their art to be influenced—and this

Cherubini says, " *C'est mon premier opéra, j'avais alors dix-neuf ans accomplis.*"
The famous male soprano Crescentini sang in this opera.

for that considerable period until Boieldieu and Auber appeared—by the characteristics of this severe apostle of the Italian School: a composer who stands out a veritable giant among Italian masters of contrapuntal art, and one who ranks with the noblest followers of Bach and Handel in the great walk of polyphonic musical art.

In the autumn of 1784, Cherubini received an invitation to visit London, *en route* to which he passed through Turin and Paris. This was in the good old days when it was the practice of Italian Opera managers not only to import renowned singers, but also to invite to this country distinguished composers, in order that works might be written expressly for the opera-house here. *Tempora mutantur!* Important events sprang from this journey. In Paris he met Viotti the violinist, and from this meeting Cherubini's long career among the French people really dates. It might have been otherwise had the people of Turin impressed him with their earnest regard, when he made, as it were, his final effort to please his own countrymen by bringing out there *Ifigenia in Aulide,* his eleventh opera.[1] Cherubini, however, placed his own value upon the smiles and applause with which the Turinese greeted this score—in which, by the way, is some of Cherubini's best music—for he returned and continued his stay in London, sensible beyond doubt of his failure in Italy; yet perchance not unmindful that a new era was dawning upon Italian musical art, when such sober and measured music had

[1] It is in this opera that Halévy discovered the first signs of Cherubini's budding genius.

perforce to give way to a less learned art—distinguished
for its exuberance of melody and most lavish vocal
fioriture—having its advent with Rossini, and the
death-knell of which we shall see will probably be
sounded with the decease of Verdi.

In London Cherubini did not cause great stir,
although George Prince of Wales noticed Cherubini,
and an appointment was obtained for him as Composer
to the King—which post Cherubini held for one year.[1]

During his stay in London he produced in succession
at the King's Theatre in the Haymarket, *La Finta
Principessa* (1785)—an opera buffa in two acts ; and
in 1786, *Il Giulio Sabino*, also in two acts, and
having a libretto by Metastasio. Both these works
were failures, for neither the *début* and singing of
Marchesi, nor the goodwill of Cherubini's royal
patrons were sufficient to float *Giulio Sabino*, which
we are told " was murdered in its birth for want of
the necessary support of the capital singers in the
principal parts."

It was in 1788 that Cherubini arrived in Paris.
Having become acquainted with Léonard, Marie An-
toinette's *coiffeur*, who had obtained permission to
found Italian opera, Cherubini was entrusted with
the musical direction. He produced *Démophon*, the
libretto of which was by Marmontel. This was on
the 5th of December.

What had remained to its composer of the light
character of the Neapolitan School, leavened even as

---

[1] It was in this capacity, probably, that he assisted at the
Handel Commemoration Festival in Westminster Abbey July,
1784.

this had been by his personal individuality, was deliberately placed aside in *Démophon*, wherein was clearly foreshadowed that grand style so soon to be found fully developed in Cherubini's next important opera. *Démophon* did not prove a success, but that it assured a brilliant future for its composer all the critics were agreed. The chief objections were that the music was cramped, dry, unequal in colour and dramatic interest. Here and there, be it recorded, a critic was found bold enough to throw a modicum of blame upon the librettist. Among such stood Fétis. "Marmontel's verses," wrote he, "were sham." It was a bad book.

Here what may be termed Cherubini's early and Italian period ends.

Now, undoubtedly, did Cherubini give signs of the great master which he was, ere long, to prove himself to be. *Démophon* failed to please, but it bore unmistakable evidence of a new vista in operatic method and style. Its thoroughly effective Overture was the first of a series, several of which, as is known, have proved ever welcome features in concert programmes. The opera itself exhibited plainly a state of artistic restlessness which could only be satisfied by uncontrolled expression. The finished detail, the majestic form, the brilliant instrumentation, the lofty style, the beautiful chorus music, all was of a new order, new from the composer, new to the public who listened to it. Failure that it was, contents and non-contents alike looked forward to a next opera with surprising anxiety.

The public had rather long to wait, for it was not until some three years afterwards that Cherubini's

thirteenth opera saw the light. Possibly Fétis's as-
sumption that the composition of *Démophon* was a
"protracted torture" for Cherubini is the correct
solution for the failure of the work. If so, the master
may well be excused for his rest.

Lodoïska was produced on the 18th of July, 1791.
In this work the higher flight was made. The
forecasts in *Démophon* assumed actual form in
Lodoïska. Cherubini here asserts himself in advanced
harmonic combinations, brilliant, nay, even startling
and realistic orchestral effects and tone colourings
which mark a great artistic advance—a stride so vast
that it is scarcely surprising that it caused alarm
among the composers of the day.

Only these three years from the production of
Démophon, and the *habitués* and others of the Salle
Feydeau at Paris had the satisfaction of witnessing
the performance of *Lodoïska* – the opera which made
Cherubini's name famous throughout Europe, and
which stamped its composer as a revolutionizer of
Italian Opera, and the reformer, if not the founder
of French Opera. Some folk went so far as to credit
him with something worse than revolutionary pro-
pensities towards the lyric drama. The outburst of
genius had at last come. If delayed, as was the case
with Gluck and Rameau—the latter wrote his first
opera when he was fifty—it was none the less determined. Nor was it an uncertain herald, for the new
work breathed the spirit of stormy times, and evidenced
clearly enough that a new era was dawning upon
musical Europe, one to be not less marked in its
effects than the changes which were overtaking all

phases of social life. Mozart, with his marvellous lyrical creations, had administered a severe blow to voluptuous dramatic music. Loved by the gods, the composer of *Don Giovanni* closed his eyes for ever in the same year that *Lodoïska*—the work of another purist—appeared to negative the approaching flood of melodic exuberance which was soon to distinguish the Rossinian period in Italian Opera.

More than this, Cherubini, like Mozart, gave fresh life to dramatic music. Music, as did other matters, languished in the Eighteenth century, and the fulness and depth which Cherubini incorporated, notably in *Lodoïska*, bore striking contrast to the flimsy and soulless compositions of the departing age. Reviewing the growth and development of lyrical art since its day, the artistic import of works, such as *Lodoïska*, Mozart's *Don Giovanni*, and operas by other giant purists, becomes more and more apparent. Without those great life-giving properties—the deep grounded musical purpose and intent, the profound learning, combined with harmonic and melodic resource, the richness of fancy and idea, the command of vocal and instrumental forms, the grasp of happy periods and great dramatic situations—all this, and more, which make up a great musical structure, had a distinct advent in the dramatic compositions of Mozart, Gluck, and Cherubini; and without such properties stage music would have reached us in pitiable garb. It is the great lyrical compositions of these masters which have made dramatic music, and which have long served to check and steady the impetus of a too exotic and voluptuous lyrical tendency.

Lodoïska fell like a thunderbolt amid the music of
the day in France. It was a well-directed effort; a
species of musical purgative; and withal an original
and masterly composition. Many of the Parisians
liked it—many did not. That it was produced nearly
two hundred times in one year was sufficient testimony
of its merits for the former; while the dissentients
were comforted with not a little adverse criticism
which the opera received. One of these critical finger-
posts was of opinion that " Cherubini had not become
worthy of being placed beside the Paisiellos, the Gug-
lielmis, and the Cimarosas, his contemporaries," going
on to say that "since it is easier to produce harmonies and noise, effects of purely theoretical calcula-
tion, than to create song, M. Cherubini, renouncing
the Italian method, which requires imagination and
fecundity, allies himself to the German manner in
substituting for an expressive melody the noisy and
often unnatural effects of instrumental profusion."

Possibly this intelligent guide was impregnated
with the creed that music to be music should consist
of all tunes, in which case the new style of music by
Cherubini, characterized as it was with a great command of theoretical device and orchestral resource,
must have proved both novel, perplexing, and disappointing !

Lodoïska supplied a further instance of the in-
different *libretti* which seemed to be the lot of this
master-mind. The story was a mixture of the
Richard Cœur de Lion and *Fidelio* elements, and
though it possessed points of interest, it was ad-
mittedly an awkward book to treat.

The plot is the usual story : Lodoïska, in love with one Floreski, is a prisoner in the castle of a more powerful suitor, Dourlinski. Floreski presents himself at the castle as brother to Lodoïska, and anxious, for the mother's sake, for the girl's return. Tyrannous Dourlinski receives him cordially, but keeps his eye upon him, with the result that Floreski is discovered drugging the soldiers who guard the precious Lodoïska. The concoction employed could have been no mean mixture, since the guards declare of it "Bon-bon," though it has brought them down with giddy heads on to the flag-stones. At this juncture occurs a catastrophe which quickly disposes of the intrigue element. The castle is stormed by the Tartars, and Dourlinski, with his mind intent probably upon more mundane things, forgets Lodoïska, with the result that the rescue of the heroine is easily established.

Between the production of *Lodoïska* and *Medée*, in which latter work Cherubini soars to the height of his operatic greatness, little of importance occurred— save, perhaps, firstly the production in December, 1794, of *Eliza*,[1] an opera with music of extreme beauty and tenderness, but having a wretched libretto ; second, the Foundation in 1795 of the Paris *Conservatoire* of Music, whereof Cherubini was appointed Inspector and Master in Counterpoint ; and lastly, Cherubini's marriage—this in 1795—to Cécile Tourette.

Of this marriage were born one son and two daughters.

Eliza, the above-mentioned opera, is in two acts.

---

[1] Madame Scio was the first *Eliza*.

The words by St. Cyr proved quite unworthy of the exceptionally beautiful music to which Cherubini wedded them. Hence has become lost to the world some of the most tender and highly dramatic music that emanated from this rich fount. The scene is laid on Mont St. Bernard. It is early morn, Prior and monks, lantern in hand, and with picks and faithful hounds, are out on the mount in quest for any lost or snow-bound travellers. A still more compassionate task, however, awaits the Prior. He learns of the disconsolate grief of one Florindo, who has been in-formed by letter of the inconstancy of his lover, Eliza. Consolation is unvailing. The Prior comforts, but Florindo will not be comforted, and, as night is ap-proaching Florinda is urged to a shelter in the hospice. The evening bell tolls, and among those whom it calls to the hospice are the voyagers Eliza and her servant Laura, accompanied by a guide. Ere she enters, Eliza faints from exhaustion. The next day the Prior engages in conversation with Eliza. Florindo's name is soon introduced, but alas, the outcome is that nothing but death can assuage his wounds. An ap-proaching storm seems to favour this. Soon the mountain is the scene of a terrible frenzy—storm, lightning and an avalanche. Amid all Florindo is espied on the edge of a precipice; a mass of falling snow sweeps Florindo and all before it. Then comes the rescue, and all ends joyously. Such briefly are the main points of the story of one of the gems of operatic construction from Cherubini's fertile pen, a work which an enterprising *impresario* might do worse than unearth for present day theatre-goers, who would, doubtless, welcome something of an operatic novelty in lieu of the worn-out Italian operas which every season again brings round.

Medée, or *Medea*, the sixteenth opera, was produced at the Feydeau Théatre on the 13th of March, 1797. It was not a success—a result that was attributed to a variety of reasons, the chief of these being that Hoffmann, the librettist, had written a weak book—a dull and heavy one it assuredly was—and that the Feydeau establishment had not the means and the staff for doing the opera and the music even moderate justice. Respecting the music the critics of the time discovered in it reminiscences of Méhul and Gluck: others expressed quite opposite views, admiring its melodies, its instrumentation, and, above all, its striking originality! None of them, however, appear to have discovered the chief objection to the opera, which is a decided monotony in its general sentiment, and a too complete centreing of the interest in the title *rôle*. And bearing in mind that in this opera, and also in *Les Deux Journées*, Cherubini forsakes more and more the melodic profuseness and rapture of Italian art, and substitutes consummate theoretical learning, combined with a nobility of strength and richness of orchestration hitherto unknown in opera, it is not surprising that the reception of *Medée* was unfavourable to Cherubini. The result, too, of an inefficient *caste* may well be imagined. The physical power necessary to sustain the part of Medea is terrific, while the whole opera is on so large a scale, and is so full of tremendous scenes that it has come to be regarded as a work "the fair execution of which is hardly possible." The grandest and most imposing dramatic music Cherubini ever wrote is to be found in *Medée*, but it makes trying demands upon soloist and chorus alike.

The Overture in the first place is a consummate work of classical art. Sir George Grove has said of it:—"The intention of the overture (to *Medée*)—doubtless designed to reflect the story, though quite independent of the opera itself—every hearer may best interpret for himself. Though a most effective composition, and as an orchestral piece of music full of beauties, it appears to the writer to belong more to the region of pure music—the overtures to the *Zauberflöte* and *Cosi Fan Tutti*—than to those more romantic and picturesque compositions of which Beethoven gave the world the earliest examples in his *Coriolan* and *Leonora*, and which Mendelssohn continued in his *Hebrides* and *Melusina*, and other grand and delightful compositions of this class. With all its power and skill, Cherubini's mind was too conservative and classical to permit of his entering on this path in the orchestra. But his overtures are so pure, so free from everything petty or commonplace, and so abounding in beauty, that while listening to them one may well be pardoned for forgetting that any school of music ever existed but that of which they form so bright and enduring an ornament."

Medée is Cherubini's greatest achievement in dramatic music. No other of the twenty-and-five operas which he composed displays the composer in so great and sublime a mood. Its grandeur and classical proportion render it a creation equal to the masterpieces of the regenerator of opera, Gluck. It is a *chef-d'œuvre* which, it may be truly said, remains unsurpassed in the domain of dramatic art. Many better known operas exist, many a lyrical production has kept the stage longer, many a more grateful vocal score is known to the singer and auditor, but as a stupendous work, both in conception and treatment, it is transcendently great, and in every respect a notable example of tragical musical drama.

The story of *Medée* is familiar to all readers of Greek tales and translations of classic legends. In the version of it as set by Cherubini, the old Greek story is sensibly weakened by undue prominence to the debased element in the story.

Medée holds the German public more than either French or English audiences. It was at the Frankfort Theatre that the late Mr. Chorley first saw it represented, and then wrote, " The opera might be objected to as one too largely made up of solos and duets, were it not for the ingenuity with which the chorus is employed to heighten and work up several of the movements, so as to conceal the monotony which else must have resulted from such a general want of complication. . . . It must be further owned that the entire part (of Medea) is written most ungraciously for the voice—that besides its merciless length and demand upon the energies, it perpetually claims qualities which are not vocal." To confirm this latter statement, the author of " Modern German Music " cites the case of Madame Scio, whose deadly complaint arose from " her singing in this very opera."

Nevertheless, there are many indescribably beautiful numbers in *Medée*. The number for bass solo and chorus in which Creon invokes a blessing on the bride and Jason, is superb in its vocal and instrumental advantages. Not less perfect is Cherubini's idea and utterance in the duet, in this same first act, for Medea and Jason. The worked-up passion is tremendous, and probably the whole annals of dramatic music do not afford a more striking instance of sustained and passionate expression than the close to this initial act in *Medée*. A similar outburst of impetuous capacity occurs in another duet for the same two personages in the second act. The most beautiful music, however, appears in the closing bridal scene of act two. Here all the stately severity of Cherubini's style serves the master. Especially is this noticeable in the fine march introduced here, which must ever rank with the best examples of such movements. The third act is the marvel of the work. It contains one of the grandest storm scenes in music's *répertoire*. As Mr. Chorley wrote:—
"From the time when *Medea* appears on the scene, in the midst of this tumult of the elements, she is never again allowed to leave the stage, the remainder of the opera consisting of two *scenas* for her, both on the grandest scale; the first with her children, the second as the triumphant Nemesis dealing destruction round her."

It was on June 6th, 1865, that *Medée* was revived at Her Majesty's Theatre under the direction of Signor Arditi, and during Mr. Mapleson's management. On this occasion the trying title *rôle* was accepted by the

—alas! now departed—famed Mdlle. Tietjens. Of the
performance the truly great critic of the *Athenæum*
wrote:—"We have never accepted Mdlle. Tietjens
as the new Tragic Muse, on whom the mantle of
Pasta and Malibran is reputed to have fallen; but
this, by much the most difficult part she has at-
tempted, is the one in which she seems, as an actress,
to approach nearer high drama than on any other
occasion. She misses, however, an opportunity in
the bridal scene, the one where Pasta's attitude of
silent vengeance maturing its full purpose was so
appalling, without the slighest disturbance of stage
effect. Her voice proves equal to the strain with
which it is loaded by Cherubini. We shall be disappointed if this does not ripen into one of her best
personations. The *Jason*, Dr. Günz, is perhaps no
more insipid than a *Jason* is permitted to be. Mr.
Santley's *Creon* (though the part is not among those
which suit his voice best) is excellent, and so is
the orchestra, and so is the chorus. The audience
was thoroughly aroused and interested. On our-
selves this superb ideal work, as coming after the
effect of the washy, flashy, trashy musical dramas
which we are invited to accept as new, is not to be
overstated. The sensation of satisfaction and excitement, not without surprise, is as strong as that
which any true lover of sculpture must feel, who,
after 'running the gauntlet' through a crowd of
fauns, dancing-girls, and other such modern furni-
ture marble-folk, finds himself looking up to Michael
Angelo's 'Pensiero' in the Medici chapel."

Much that Mr. Chorley wrote a quarter of a century ago is applicable to-day. Amid much boasted musical progress, melodic exuberance and audacity, unctuous harmony, and general surface matter in all directions is the prevailing thing at the opera-house. *Lohengrin* and *Tannhäuser* are trustworthy 'draws,' but where is the manager nowadays with the courage to substitute *Medée* for *Il Trovatore* or the *Sonnambula?*

Passing over *L'Hôtellerie Portugaise*, a one-act opera, produced on July 25th, 1798, and *La Punition* (1799), we come to *Les Deux Journées*, in which work its fertile composer is seen in his happiest mood as an opera composer.

Les Deux Journées was first represented at the Feydeau Théatre on January 16th, 1800. It was unanimously declared to be a masterpiece of lyric drama, and the Parisian *connoisseurs* raved over its incomparable music. It saw some two hundred representations ere the public admiration even cooled, and then the opera went the round of all the European capitals, while in Germany, where it became known as *Der Wasserträger*, it took a firm hold. The libretto has always been the admiration of musicians—even of Mendelssohn, who was most fastidious in the matter of *libretti.*

The story of the libretto is a very interesting one, and relates the expedients of a persecuted President of the French Parliament, who is befriended in his escapes by a kindly water-carrier. The scene is laid in Paris, and in the village of Gonesse, and the time is 1647.

From a musical and literary point of view, success

was deserved. The libretto by Bouilly was at once well chosen, carefully treated, and distinctly interesting; indeed, Goethe looked upon it as a model comic opera book. Musically it was a stroke of real genius. As has been well said, the composition presented so many particular beauties, such great perfection, that it at once took its rank as a classical work. . . . The most famous composers studied it, and Beethoven used always to keep the score by him on his table.

Doubtless *Les Deux Journées* is a more agreeable opera than *Medée*, to which it stands in bold contrast. Here Cherubini subjugates his severe style with its decorous moderation in melody and feeling, for a sphere of art so natural, so *suave* that even the untutored ear is tempted to linger long over the arias and couplets in this idyllic drama. So genial is Cherubini, as we here find him, making concessions to beauty of sound and allowing his severer muse to give way to a less formal one with more warmth of feeling and passionate expression, that it might be regretted that the classic composer did not labour more in the realm of melodic fancy and artistic *abandon*. Nothing could exceed the ease and grace of the melodies in this opera, while their charm and vocal aptness are a sufficient argument against the assertions of those who are in the habit of contending that Cherubini could not write for the voice. Of the general musical perfection of *Il Portator d'Acqua* (by which title the same opera is known in Italy), of all the richness of its magnificent instrumentation, its brilliant orchestration, of its wealth of scientific form and detail, it would be impossible to speak too highly. Such a diorama of tone may well be likened to the unveiling of a glorious Paul Veronese.

The best of criticism has always been in favour of *Les Deux Journées*. Schlüter says, "The music itself is perfect, being equally distinguished for tenderness and expressiveness as for noble simplicity and purity of form." Fétis writes, "There is a copiousness of melody in Cherubini, especially in the *Deux Journées ;* but such is the richness of the accompanying harmony, and the brilliant colouring of the instrumentation considering the period when the work appeared ; such, above all, was the inability of the leaders of the public taste to appreciate at that time the combination of all these beauties, that the merit of the melody was not appreciated at its just value." Weber has said, "The opera displays a pleasing richness of melody, vigorous declamation, and all-striking truth in the treatment of the situations, ever new, ever heard and retained with pleasure." A more modern writer (Ritter), speaking of *Les Deux Journées* and Cherubini's other operas, declares "they will remain for the earnest student a classic source of exquisite artistic enjoyment, and serve as models of a perfect mastery over the deepest resources and means that the rich field of musical art presents."

One great advance Cherubini effected in *Les Deux Journées*. He hit hard at the accepted operatic system —musical dramas composed of airs from beginning to end. The whole of this fascinating score was composed (with the exception of a duet and canzonet) of concerted pieces and choruses, all strong and vigorous in character, and strikingly beautiful in harmonial mould and orchestral colouring.

Spohr's testimony to the beauties of this work runs thus :—"I recollect when the *Deux Journées* was performed for the first time, how, intoxicated with delight and the powerful impression that the work had made on me, I asked on that very evening to have the score given to me, and sat over it the whole night, and that it was that opera chiefly that gave me the first impulse to composition."

The introduction in E major to the Overture of *Les Deux Journées* is a piece of music which has always commanded the admiration of good critics. That excellent judge, the late Professor John Ella, says of it,—

"To my mind there is no more striking effect of powerful imagination suggestive of the darkest imagery of tragic incidents than the whole of the introduction to *Les Deux Journées*. After the two lovely cadences of serene placid harmony, come the basses with powerful unisons in a grand figure of a vague character reposing on a deep pedal note. How touching are the bewailing short melodic phrases so tenderly expressed, with the penetrating chord of the augmented fifth in its simple structure! The mysterious tremolo of the violins, the wailing effect of the flutes, the tragic responses of the basses, and the terrific utterance of the corni ff in the fifth of the dominant, until the grand climax of the allegro, are in the highest degree suggestive, and have served Weber and Mendelssohn to good purpose. This introduction I have always considered one of the most poetical creations of Cherubini." Subjoined are a few bars which will help the mind towards an appreciation of the enthusiastic vein of the author of "Musical Sketches: Abroad and at Home," in his admiration of this masterly Introductory movement :—

a. Figure for basses in unison.
b. Melodic phrases.
c. Tremolo of the violins.
d. Responses of the basses.

It was on Thursday, the 20th of June, 1872, that an Italian version of this masterpiece by Cherubini (under the title *I Due Giornate*) was produced in

London at Drury Lane Theatre under the direction of that unrivalled *chef d'orchestra*, the late Sir Michael Costa. The *caste* included Mdlle. Tietjens as *Constance*, Mdlle. Roze as *Marcellina*, Mdlle. Bauermeister filled the part of *Angelina*, Signor Agnesi was the "Water-carrier," Signor Rinaldini *Antonio*, while Signor Foli played the *rôle* of the Commander.

With such a company—alas! how few remain—a magnificent rendering was inevitable—and this proved to be the issue. The singing and acting of Mdlle. Tietjens was never surpassed by any previous representations, and her efforts alone seemed to ensure a wide popularity for the work in this country. Every one was enthusiastic. "The expressions of admiration on the part of the public," wrote the talented critic of the *Athenæum*, "were palpable and audible enough ; and in the corridors, and in the *foyer*, ordinarily cold and self-possessed musicians declared their enthusiastic appreciation of the work, of the masterly accompaniments of Sir Michael Costa for the dialogue and action, and of its extraordinarily fine execution."

Yet a scare was got up ! A few daily-paper critics told the public that the story was too simple, and the music too learned ; it was suggested that the opera would not 'draw.' The alarm was taken up, and finally Mr. Mapleson, as *impresario*, had no other course open to him other than that of withdrawing a work which did not commend itself to the leaders of popular musical opinion !

An important opera that followed *Les Deux Journées* was *Anacréon*,[1] the libretto of which was furnished by

---

[1] The full title to this work is *Anacréon, ou l'Amour fugitif*.

one Mendouze, who, judging from the book in question, had not acquired the art of writing successful librettos.

Anacréon was first represented at the Grand Opéra on the 4th of October, 1803, and, surviving for a while, died an early death. Mr. Bellasis, in his " Memorials of Cherubini," states that " Cherubini, in a private letter, attributed the failure of the work *à la clique infernale acharnée contre tous ceux qui font partie du Conservatoire.*" It is not less probable, however, that the popular opinion as to the heavy character of the *Anacréon* music was the real cause of the failure. In fact, the generous music—the happy style and colouring, so profuse in *Les Deux Journées*—had not been maintained in *Anacréon*. The music of the latter reflected, perhaps, too faithfully the mind and disposition of its maker. Cherubini was unhappy at this time. He had had two or three collisions with Napoleon, and was gloomy and disappointed. So, too, was his music moody and unsatisfactory.

Yet the work possessed some beauties. There is the magnificent Overture—a model of what overtures should be—full of rich melody, supported by striking and original combinations of the tone art.[1] All the choruses of the opera are concise and replete with effect ; while it would be difficult to find music to surpass the beauty, the elegance, and originality of such numbers as the trio " *Dans ma verte et*

---

[1] Cherubini impressed the Overture form. It is in the *Anacréon* Overture that he secures a grand effect by originating the long and gradual crescendo, thus anticipating a similar expedient by Rossini.

belle jeunesse," and the quartet *" Des nos cœurs pars."*

Nevertheless, Cherubini's fame continued to spread. His music had carried his name far and wide, and in Germany especially had it met with every appreciation. It is scarcely surprising, therefore, to find him the recipient of an invitation to compose an opera for Vienna—the then great seat of the musical world—an invitation coupled with the request that he would conduct it personally.

Faniska, an opera in three acts, was the result of this commission, and the work was represented for the first time at the Kärnthnerthor Theatre on the 25th of February, 1806, not alone before the Emperor Francis Joseph II. and his splendid Court, but before Beethoven and Haydn, whom historians tell us pushed in among the crowd that they too might hear the music and strains of him whom they regarded so highly, and to whose unrivalled power and learning they were not ashamed to bear witness. "I am very old," exclaimed the aged Father of Symphony as he embraced Cherubini, "but I am your son."

Nothing could have been more spontaneous than the success which *Faniska* achieved. Every one liked it—the critics, the Viennese musicians, French composers, the Italian melodists, the occupants of the stalls and boxes, and even the gallery censors were unanimous in their praise. "The magnificent music," wrote one reviewer, "excited the admiration of all competent critics."

The story of *Faniska* runs thus :—In one of the convulsions which have desolated Poland, *Faniska* and her infant daughter are seized and imprisoned in the castle of *Count Zamoski*. The fortunate jailor is, of course, *selon les règles*, deeply enamoured of his captive, and also, of course, finds her deaf to his most earnest entreaties. As a last resource, he determines to impress her with the belief that her husband is dead. *Rasinski*, who, in disguise, is hovering round his rival's castle, offers to become himself the messenger of his own decease, and is introduced for that purpose to the lady. He meets his wife with firmness, and delivers to her his own portrait as the proof of his veracity, when the infantine caresses of his daughter cause him to betray himself, and he is forthwith consigned to a dungeon, with the not comfortable assurance of meeting, on the morrow, the fate of a traitor. This ends the first act. The second and third are occupied by the usual intrigues and expedients to work his liberation, which is at length effected; his party storm the castle, *Zamoski* falls, and the husband and wife are again united.

Faniska is a triumph of musical art. Its magnificent Overture, so well known, is frequently allotted a place in concert programmes, and any comment upon it would be superfluous. Nor is the rest of the music less masterly or less deserving of popularity, for there is much in *Faniska* equal to anything Cherubini has written. Of the most varied and beautiful character, abounding with charming points of imitation and graceful contrapuntal learning, rich with choice harmonies and ever-varying tints of tone and orchestral colour, the music may be said to show

Cherubini in his happiest mood. If it is not an error of judgment to quote individual examples where all the numbers are almost past description, special stress might be placed upon the exquisite and thoroughly characteristic aria, an early number in the opera, for Zamoski, the bass—a song in E flat which should be in the *répertoire* of every bass singer with a good compass, and a desire to possess a thoroughly characteristic excerpt by this classic composer. In the next number occurs the expressive *Preghiera 'Eterno Iddio,'* "of which," says a writer in the *Harmonicon,* "it is hardly too much to say, that, for variety of modulation and just expression, it yields only to the great scene in *Don Giovanni,* where *Donna Anna* mourns over the dead body of her murdered parent, and incites her lover to revenge his death." The accompaniment for the three *violoncelli* to this prayer, and the interspersed passages for the oboe and flute, are wedded to the song in the happiest manner. Other equally interesting numbers are a duet for *Faniska* and *Rasinski;* a beautiful Romance in G minor, —both in the second act.

All the choruses are spirited and harmonious, and the military music in the third act is exceedingly clever. As a whole the work is in every sense worthy a place on modern opera boards, and it must always rank as one of the finest contributions to the lyric drama.

Cherubini still clung to dramatic art. As a matter of fact it was not profitable to him in a pecuniary sense, but he was at least making himself heard and felt through its channel.

Hence, following *Faniska* came *Pimmalione*,[1] in one act, represented, as the work of an anonymous composer, before the Emperor Napoleon I. at the Château des Tuileries Théatre (1809) ; *Le Crescendo*,[2] an opera of little interest (1810); when we come to *Les Abencérages*[3] —the libretto of which was written by Jouy. On the 6th of April, 1813, the work was given at the Grand Opéra, but without success, although the Parisians admired the music and the treatment of the poor libretto.

As to the beauty of the music, Mendelssohn bore testimony many years afterwards. "I've got his (Cherubini's) *Abencérages*," wrote the last of the Titans of music, "and cannot sufficiently admire the sparkling fire, the clever original phrasing, the extraordinary delicacy and refinement with which the whole is written, or feel grateful enough to the grand old man for it. Besides, it is all so free."

The Overture to *Les Abencérages*, so obscure in several parts, has been well likened to the sun disengaging itself with difficulty from the clouds enveloping it. Reference is made to this Overture in a number of the "Quarterly Musical Magazine," a publication which it is to be regretted came to a

---

[1] Napoleon was moved to tears by the music of this opera. His bearing towards its composer remained, however, unaltered.

[2] In this opera is a remarkable song rendered by a being who dislikes any sort of noise. Consequently the air, which is descriptive of a combat, is sung *sotto voce* to a very soft accompaniment.

[3] The attention of the Parisian public was diverted from this opera by the disastrous news of the French retreat from Moscow.

discontinuance. There F. W. H. says, "The least attractive of any Cherubini has written, this overture still contains many indubitable proofs of the ability which may be found more fully displayed in the others."

Ali Baba,[1] the last and twenty-fifth of Cherubini's operas, and which has the merit of being the longest he wrote, contained no less than a thousand pages of manuscript—so long, in fact, that the Paris publishers declined to print the whole of the MS. It appeared in 1833, or twenty years after *Les Abencérages*, being first represented at the *Académie de Musique* on the 22nd July. It is probably the tamest of Cherubini's mature period compositions for the lyric stage, possessing little or no individuality, replete with sheer learning and antiquated scholarship, but quite devoid of inspired or beautiful music. The history of the score as given by Cherubini is this:—"An opera which I began long ago (this was in 1783, when it bore the title *Kourkourgi*) in three acts, and which I finished in four acts, with a prologue."

This work proved yet another failure. More anxious for his reputation in his old than he had ever been in his young days, Cherubini did not forget to paper the pit of the theatre, whither he sent many of his *Conservatoire* scholars. They found an enemy there in the person of Berlioz. "Ere the first act was over," Berlioz says, "I was so disappointed at not having heard something new, that I could not restrain myself from muttering loud enough to be heard by

---

Also named *Hali Baba; ou les Quarante Voleurs.*

those around me, 'Twenty francs for an idea!' In
the second act I increased my bid—'Forty francs for
an idea!' The *finale* began, and the same tame music
continued. 'There!' I exclaimed, 'eighty francs
for an idea!' The *finale* over, I rose up, exclaiming,
'Ah, my faith! I am not rich enough—I give it
up!'"

As for Cherubini, "He," writes one of his biographers,
"after the last general rehearsal left for Versailles,
having carefully calculated beforehand the duration of
the acts and *entr'actes*. When the clock at the palace
of Versailles struck eight o'clock in the evening of the
day of *Ali Baba's* first representation, Cherubini
pulled put his watch and said, '*Maintenant ou commence
l'ouverture.*' At every hour, or rather at every act,
he looked at his watch. At half-past eleven *Ali Baba*
was over according to his watch, 'Which,' said he,
'*allait tres bien, et marquait l'heure de l'opéra.*'"

The old man then went to bed and slept peacefully,
but did not return to Paris until he had received a
re-assuring dispatch, and never once went to see *Ali
Baba* performed.

The public all but snored over *Ali Baba,* and the
strong-minded openly vowed it to be the last effort of
a grand old man. One account says, "In *Ali Baba*
everything was wearisome and suporific—poem, music,
and ballet. Those fastidious forty thieves had better
rested eternally buried in their jars and in the works
of Galland. . . *Ali Baba* is one of those fossilized
operas which a director only accepts when they are
thrust down his throat by illustrious old age. . . .
The public yawned so much and so widely under *Ali*

D

Baba's very nose, that real hissing would have spoken less eloquently."

A more favourable criticism was to the effect that, "All competent judges were lost in astonishment at the fact of a composer, whose first works bore the date of 1771, being able sixty years later to produce another of such extraordinary freshness and such glowing fancy. . . . His latest dramatic production displayed, in conjunction with the maturest knowledge and the most beautiful form, the loveliest blossoms of profound feeling and youthful passion."

*　　*　　*　　*　　*

Here, then, we leave Cherubini as a composer for the lyric stage. His most fervent admirers could hardly style him a successful opera composer, or one who, despite all that he did, had permanently influenced the style of any school of operatic music, not even the French school, to which he allied himself more than any other. He certainly gave an appreciable impetus to French opera, but those very qualities most characteristic of Cherubini's music were least calculated to make it popular with the French people.

The Parisians were by no means insensible to his magnificent musical *ensembles*, or to the means employed in securing these, but his pure classicism never went down deep into their hearts, and the first tolerable music-maker that came by—Auber, to wit—transplanted him in their affections. This was poor gratitude to the man who, if he did not permanently influence the style of, yet raised the lyric drama in France to an importance as a social necessity far beyond that at which he found it; who, we might say, created

Méhul, Lesueur, Spontini, and Halévy; and who gave
a spurt to musical art generally, at a critical moment
such as has fallen to the lot of few other musicians to
give.

It is scarcely a pleasant task to reflect upon the dramatic music side of Cherubini's career. It was marked
by many vicissitudes—personal, political, and profes-
sional. For over thirty years—for such is the space
between *Il Quinto Fabio* of 1780 and *Les Abencérages*
of 1813—the champion of purity and dignity in art
had laboured in the cause of stage music. A reasonable expectation—and one which every lover of truth
in conception and expression would expect to have seen
realized—would have been a steady and ever-increasing
success, work by work. But such a progressive experience was not the portion of this son of art. A
missionary of classic doctrine, his ideal standard was
not understood of the people; the soil of France was no
congenial one for such a teaching, whether by precept
or example. The temper of the public was towards
a lively strain. Ear-tickling music was the order
preferred, and the aural senses were so pledged that
the persistent teachings of Cherubini were not of
efficacy enough to wean ear and mind to a sound
lyrical perception.

It is easy to see the lyrical purpose of Cherubini.
He had in mind the development of the highest form
of grand opera for France. Gluck's reforms and aims
needed to be carried on, and Cherubini determined to
do this. Despite obstacle, he accomplished his task,
although it proved an unprofitable labour for himself,
and has been apparently of little lasting art advantage

to subsequent dramatic music in France. As a German musical writer[1] says, " While Cherubini carried out, in the melody, the fundamental law of dramatic truth, the agreement of the music with the situations in the drama, and their poetic expression, as laid down by Gluck, he exhibited greater depth of intention, fuller and bolder harmony, and a style of instrumentation which, by its richness, and the characteristic employment of the wind instruments especially, in conformity with the peculiar quality of their sound, introduced the orchestra in a brilliant manner, not only as the foundation for the vocal portion, but also as its necessary adjunct, and its equal in bringing about the theatrical effect as a whole."

The first notable indication of the new and grand style was seen in *Démophon*, wherein, as Picchianti says, " Cherubini exhibited a more elaborate workmanship, more grandeur of form, and so suddenly perfected his style, that he rose above the ordinary and popular intelligence of the time. . . . Only to those who thoroughly understood him was it given to foresee what a brilliant future for the French lyric stage the new composer was preparing." A beautiful number of this comparatively unknown score is the chorus, '*Ah! vous rendez la vie*,' the pure character of which, its vocal aptness, its bright and skilful orchestration, render it one of the gems of truly original musical conception, an excerpt thoroughly characteristic of the new-style music which Cherubini desired for France.

[1] In the *Niederrheinische Musik Zeitung.*

With this first step, however, came an unfortunate coincidence. The public was interested in another *Démophon* by another composer—Vogel, a Bohemian spirit who expired on the eve of the production of his finished work. Thus attention was withdrawn or refused to Cherubini's original score.

Undaunted, Cherubini made a still further effort. In *Lodoïska* he boldly assailed French music, and originated that music of effect (*musique d'effet*) which has marked subsequent opera.

This inspiration, this higher flight, was entirely his own, and the army of adherents which the style has had—Méhul, Berton, Steibelt, Lesueur, Grétry, Auber, Boieldieu, and later on, Meyerbeer and Rossini —is ample proof of the importance of the path opened out in France by this pioneer composer. Mozart (1756-1791) had accomplished much by way of grand vocal and orchestral effect in his glorious creations—the *Figaro* and *Don Giovanni* operas, but the Salzburg master's scores could scarcely have been at the service of Cherubini. *Lodoïska* appeared in the same year that Mozart died, and music of to-day probably owes more than is generally supposed to the bearing it exercised upon subsequent French musical activity.

The great and original art standard reached by Cherubini in *Lodoïska* was maintained in subsequent scores, notably in *Medée* and *Les Deux Journées*, but withal Cherubini remained to the end of his operatic career without the attainment of popular success.

To what may this be ascribed? First, Cherubini was far in advance of his age, late as this was. What

would France, what could Europe not now do for
such a genius? A giant harmonist, able to gather
together the ruins of German, French, and Italian
dramatic art forms, and restore them in reasonable
and more rational mould than did Wagne r—had
Cherubini lived in the latter half of the Nineteenth
century, a consistent lyrical representation might to-
day be before the leading capitals of Europe. For his
day Cherubini was too learned. Musicians understood
him, but the people at large did not. As for the
musical critics, they, as usual, were for and against.
There was too much originality in Cherubini for the
age. His second opera startled the people, and even
friends staggered over his measured melody and
studied harmonies. "Too learned!" was the judgment pronounced as far back as the production of
Adriano. *Démophon* was received as dry and con-
strained, and though Halévy could admire its instrumentation, and Picchianti was enabled to trace its
" masculine beauties," the public remained unappre-
ciative. Much the same charges attended his other
operas.

Secondly, another disturbing element for the success
of Cherubini in the walk of dramatic art was the
political disruptions which engaged France. A decade
such as that between the years 1790 and 1800 was
no favourable one for a musician to plant a standard.
Political feeling over-rode everything, all was per-
vaded with it. Bloodshed and terror united in 1793,
and when Louis the Sixteenth mounted the scaffold in
the Place de Louis Quinze, Cherubini lay hid in a
Carthusian monastery near Rouen. Ill luck sur-

rounded him, too, soon after the production of
Faniska.

With wife and family he had repaired to the
Austrian capital in 1805, but scarcely had the praises
of Haydn and Beethoven concerning *Faniska* been
uttered, than France and Austria were at war. With
the French troops in the palace gardens of Francis II.,
all hopes and any fruits of success were deferred. Thus
for a long time in his career France was no home for
the successful exercise of Cherubini's artist mind. It
was no advantage to him to be forced into the National Guard; to have his friends and few patrons
scattered and expatriated; at times forced to be present at scaffold scenes and executions; at one time
obliged to compose Republican songs, at others com-
pelled to administer to the musical cravings of King
or Consul.

If we seek for further explanations for his com-
parative failure as an opera composer, it will not be
denied that he was singularly unfortunate in the
selection of his *libretti*. Again, he was not a born
Frenchman, and to fail at times in marrying beautiful
music to an unmusical language is a fault which may
be easily condoned.

Cherubini's muse is neither French, nor German,
nor Italian, and it is not surprising that so far as the
French lyric stage is concerned, it had to make way
for the more dainty and piquant melody and harmony
that came in with Boieldieu, Auber, and others.
Nevertheless, Cherubini will always command a place
in opera history. His *Medée*, grand and dramatic
in the extreme; *Les Deux Journées*, in which he is

found in his most genial mood, these are works which may, in the caprice of fashion, give place to *Tannhäuser* and *La Favorita*, but they will assuredly have their turn when the public tires—as it seems already to be doing—of persevered recitative, and of that even worse affliction, the hackneyed melodies of enfeebled Italian opera.

Unhappily for Cherubini he does not find the unanimous approval of vocalists. Singers urge that he has not written vocal, much less grateful music for the voice, but it would be probably less libellous to say that he declines to orchestrate favourably for the singer; for Cherubini has a manner of finding a melody, and of wedding it to more than enough of the mathematical of contrapuntal art, and to singers accustomed to the suave tunes of Mozart, and to the instrumentally supported melodies of Rossini and Verdi, a liberal dose of contrapuntal finish and detail would be calculated to prove distasteful. Yet this must be the full measure of the charge. Cherubini is invariably happy in his instrumental combinations and selections, though at times he may overclothe his melodies.

Here, however, the man's mission asserts itself. He was born to be a composer of symphonies rather than of operas, to make instruments speak, not men, and it is to be regretted that he missed his way as a symphonist. Cherubini's name can, however, never be dissociated from any history of the orchestra. He could wield with a strong hand, and in all his musical effects, whether in the delicate combination of a string quartet, or amid the majesty of a full

orchestral movement, Cherubini's vigour never flags,
his originality constantly establishes itself, and the
harmonic and melodic element leave nothing to be
desired. He strikes decisively. There are no uncertain effects. All is sharp and firmly cut as the outline
of a Grecian marble. And, if we pause for a while
to dwell upon the exquisite finish which the master
gives to his work, every line, whether in a simple
phrase or vast movement, is distinguished by a fine
and skilful perception, which could only be possible
in the work of one gifted with a rare and keen sense
of what is poetic and beautiful.

Especially in Cherubini's Overtures are the characteristics of his classic style fully incorporated and
evident; and of such overtures those to *Medée, Anacréon,* and *Les Deux Journées* will live as long as
music lasts. "They," says Schlüter, "are replete
with vigour and character, their admirably drawn
outline, exquisite finish, and instrumentation cause
them to be reckoned as models of their kind."

A SACRED MUSIC COMPOSER.

IF Cherubini has not covered himself with glory in his Operatic works he has won an immortal fame through his Sacred music—his Masses, Requiems, Litanies, and numerous minor compositions for the service of the Roman Church. This latter art work is marked with a strong individuality, and is of an artistic merit that will secure for it an enduring appreciation from all lovers of Church music.

Just as Handel, worn out with failure and disappointment as a composer of opera, turned, when well into life to sacred art, by which act the world was enriched by such immortal oratorios as the "Messiah," "Israel in Egypt," "Judas Maccabæus," and others, so Cherubini's career furnishes us with something of a parallel experience. His operatic career had, too, ended in failure. His emoluments had not increased ; Napoleon steadily refused him recognition or profitable post; little else seemed to await the master but a continuance of the injustice and tardy encouragement which had already led to so slow an advancement. Disgusted and disappointed, he sought relief in the quiet country home of a friend. This slight episode in his career led to a complete change in his artistic aims, and attracted him at the age of nearly fifty to the grand realm of sacred musical art.

Here we meet Cherubini at his best. His great gifts were a power of exciting and of stimulating emotion, together with an unusual capacity for the theoretical side of his art. For the exercise of the latter of these qualities the field of Church music proved an eminently favourable domain. Here he was free to develop his masterly contrapuntal skill, far more suited to Church than to Opera music, while the lack of sustained and romantic melody would be less apparent in the grandest *credo* or *gloria* than in the meanest of operas.

Thus it cannot be doubted that Cherubini is seen at most advantage in his sacred music, which will live long after his works for the lyric stage. It marks a new epoch in Roman Church music, and goes far to prove that it *is* possible for sacred music to be something other than stagey and theatrical, however dramatic it may be, and that the highest resources of art can be so employed as to conduce to a right spirit of devotion, arousing and elevating the prayerful soul rather than hindering or distracting it in the contemplation of things holy.

"Cherubini," writes a Father of the Roman Church, "possessed a remarkable aptitude for rendering sensible, for interpreting religious truths, and when we hear his music we understand that this harmonious language, so sublime, so persuasive, is not made for the holy temples, but for our intercourse with heaven."

Picchianti says : "Cherubini created a new kind of religious music which had nothing in common with anything that had been produced before."

This is agreed. The Church of his creed is greatly indebted to him. His music is a priceless enrichment to the Catholic Church—Cherubini is as a Raphael and Angelo thereto.

Certain critics have accused Cherubini of being over dramatic in his sacred compositions. Judging his music by the side of the church music of Palestrina, Carissimi, Allegri, Marcello, and such *maestri*, the charge might be supported; but Cherubini had a higher mission than these, his predecessors. They had divested their sacred music of every vestige of warm colouring, and, as Fétis says, they had treated it "as an emanation of pure sentiment, stripped of all human passion." The structure which they had reared was, indeed, finely conceived, pure in its style, and severely correct, but its walls were bare and it needed colour, it wanted life and emotional effects. It was the mission of Cherubini to supply such deficiencies. The Florentine stepped in, and showed how possible it was to blend the severe beauties of counterpoint and fugue with dramatic expression, sustained by every wealth of instrumentation. As he gave soul, expression, and feeling to Opera, so he did to Mass and *Credo*.

Cherubini's first important Mass, the one in F for three voices and orchestra, properly catalogued as No. 4 (the earlier numbered masses being reckoned as juvenile compositions), was brought to light in the year 1809. In the autumn of that year Cherubini was seeking repose in the quiet village of Chimay,[1]

---

[1] Here was the residence of M. le Prince de Chimay, whither Cherubini had been invited to rest and recruit—a guest of the cultured owner of the castle.

and there it was that the Kyrie[1] and Gloria of this fine work were first performed, and this with perhaps the poorest array of talent that Cherubini had ever met.

Cherubini had dropped music, and was given over for a season to his favourite pursuit of botany. The collecting of specimens of the vegetable kingdom, an inquiry into their growth and natural history, afforded him a pleasurable occupation, and one which he entered into with his usual ardent spirit. It was at this time that the project was formed in the village for performing a mass with music in Chimay Church. All available throats and lungs were ready to get up the music, but—this was not in existence! In their plight they had recourse to Cherubini, who considered, then refused, considered again, and finally consented. Putting aside specimens of plants and roots, he turned on to the composition of a three-voice Mass. The movements required were duly completed, and performed on the day of the long-looked-for festival.

For the voices there was a village choir, and the full instrumental strength was not more formidable than one bassoon, a single flute, two horns, two clarionets, and a string quartet.

With so unpretentious an orchestra it is somewhat surprising that the performance proved an adequate musical offering to St. Cecilia, in whose honour it was arranged. Yet the Patroness of Music appears to have been kind, and altogether so favourable an impression was left upon Cherubini, that he was subsequently

[1] Some writers say this *Kyrie* was written in the billiard-room at the castle during the playing of pool and billiards.

induced to extend and to complete the score which had been executed in part only by these villagers— the natives of Chimay.

A performance of the completed Mass took place shortly afterwards at the Hôtel de Babylon in Paris,[1] when the instrumental parts were rendered by men of accepted talent and ability. The Mass was received with enthusiasm by the *dilettanti* who crowded the *salon* of Prince de Chimay's town residence, and connoisseurs pronounced it a masterpiece, the first work of a new era in the annals of sacred musical art.

A detailed description of this fine contribution to Roman Church music will be to many unnecessary. It is not Cherubini's greatest and most famous work, his Requiem Mass in C minor being held to bear that honour; while some admirers of the master refer to the D minor Requiem as his *chef-d'œuvre ;* also in some respects the F Mass music must give way to that masterly composition, the Mass in A (to be spoken of further on), so concise, finely conceived, and eminently beautiful in its melody, harmony, and general design.

It is nevertheless a grand effort, this F Mass. Its general treatment, its devotional character, its learning, the originality and exquisite beauty of much of the music make it worthy to rank with similar art forms by Haydn, Mozart, and Beethoven. Fétis declares it to be so remarkable for originality of idea and perfection of style, as to be superior to the masses by these masters. The *Kyrie* of 200 bars length abounds in beautiful music of a suppressed emotional

---

[1] This was in 1809.

character—not heavily orchestrated, but delicately and charmingly accompanied, and abounding in varied and choice devices of the contrapuntal art. The *Credo*, grand in its conception, and with music bold and vigorous enough especially in the emphatic passages of the text, is well calculated to stimulate the believer. In the *Incarnatus* and *Crucifixus* this character is changed. Love beyond expression, tenderness, and deep religious fervour prevail upon the worshipper, and concentrate the mind upon this supreme point of doctrinal acceptance.

Not less masterly is the *Allegro* movement wherein Christ's Resurrection is depicted, and this movement is followed by a fugue, so strong in subject and character, and worked out in so masterly a fashion as to form a brilliant *finale* to this setting of the Creed. *The Sanctus* of 105 bars length, well conceived and replete with beautiful and melodious music, has a religious and a subdued colouring throughout, and it would serve well as a model to modern church musicians, who in seeking after effect too often lose sight of the very words, to say nothing of the spirit, of their text. The *Agnus Dei* and *Gloria* are correspondingly treated, and are worthy in all respects of the other grand music of this Mass—a work which is specially important as being the first, if not the finest sacred work of Cherubini's Third or mature period in composition.

Concerning this Mass it has been said—" The prevailing idea in this effort has nothing in common with that which pervades all the music of the ancient Roman school; that was conceived as an emanation of

pure sentiment, apart from all human passion; while
Cherubini, on the contrary, chose that his music should
express a dramatic sense of the words, and in the
fulfilment of this idea, he gave proof of a talent so
exalted as to leave him without rival in this particular."

Passing over such works as the *Litanie della
Vergine* for four voices with instruments—written for
His Highness Prince Esterhazy de Galanta, a part of
a *Cantata*, various Romances and other small pieces,
we come to the year 1811, famous as being that in
which Cherubini composed his grand Mass in D
minor.

This Mass, if not Cherubini's *chef-d'œuvre*, is one of
the most masterly results ever obtained in the field
of sacred composition. Written [1] for four voices and
full orchestra, it is some 260 pages of score in length
—and this circumstance is an unfortunate one, since
it must ever seriously prejudice the frequent performance of this fine work in its entirety.

What prompted Cherubini to compose a Mass which
is one of the longest—indeed the longest ever written,
is difficult to conceive. [2] Certainly it cannot be urged
that Cherubini had no other means of display.
Whether we look at the music of the D minor Mass,
and judge it as music *per se*, or regard the work
from the standpoint of its conception, its originality,
its well-planned and well-executed design, the mind is

---

[1] This Mass was begun at the end of March and finished
7th October, 1811.

[2] It contains 2563 bars of music. Beethoven's longest
Mass—the celebrated D major—consists of 1929 bars.

equally impressed. Musically and technically it is surpassed by no similar work by any other master.

The Kyrie[1] is divided into three sections, which combine to constitute one of the grandest settings of these words of the Roman service. True, there are frequent repetitions of passages, the same sentiment is over and over again expressed; subject succeeds subject with almost dangerous frequency, and yet, when Cherubini gathers together these forces, a vast musical structure is the result. The three sections blend into a perfect whole—gorgeous in its instrumental colouring, rich in flow of melody, and as chaste and rare in its detail as the severest theorist could desire. There is grandeur, strength, and depth, and these qualities are not acquired to the exclusion of appropriate sentiment, varied harmony, or original thought and treatment. Nor has Cherubini lost sight of the fit character of a *Kyrie Eleison*. From beginning to end this movement in the D minor Mass is one long musical prayer—a plea for divine mercy, beautifully yet devoutly expressed, and not less reverential in character because of the gorgeous musical apparel in which it is clothed; for in his sacred music, Cherubini rarely, if ever, allows his art to exceed its legitimate mission—that of impelling and encouraging the worshipper, stimulating such an one in his religious aspirations, rather than seeking to chain him to consideration of sounds of man's creating.

In the third movement of this Kyrie (in common time, *allegro moderato*) Cherubini has introduced a

[1] 437 bars in length.

fugue in the most successful manner—not a
boisterous example of this form of writing, but one
so appropriately worked out, with voices and instruments so well kept under, and with the sentiment
and colouring so truly compatible with the religious
situation, that the most devout worshipper could
suffer no disturbance.

The *Gloria* [1] is not less finely conceived. Its brilliant
and effective opening, followed by the striking contrast
on the words, "And in earth peace," could scarcely
fail to arrest the attention, while to any willing listener,
and still more to the devout mind, sensible to
musical form and beauty, it would appeal with particular impressiveness. The singular beauty, too, of
the *Qui Tollis* and *Quoniam* carries them out of the
region of pen and ink description. The music wedded
to these is music which must last as long, at least, as
there is vitality in the Roman Church.

The *Credo*—668 bars in length—is the musical
climax of the work. In it are all the qualities which
combine to make a grand conception—well balanced
change of movement, happily judged variety both
in colour and sentiment, alterations in time and key,
consummate contrapuntal form both broad and in
detail, all this carried on by a current of pure melody,
superbly harmonized, and sustaining a pent-up interest
until the final chord. Great, too, as is the general
interest, Cherubini in the *Incarnatus* movement even
heightens the normal effect, tiding over this solemn
part of the *Credo* with consummate skill. In the

---

895 bars in length.

Crucifixus the mighty master produces a beautiful effect by a sustained unison passage for the voices on E, supported by a delicate and weird accompaniment from the violins muted. The endorsing " Amen " is the signal for a great point. On this word Cherubini builds a noble fugue. The giant theorist, never at a loss for a fugal subject, has here surpassed himself in finding the initial bars of a fugue, which, well worked out as it is, forms a fitting conclusion to an eminently grand setting of this portion of the Mass.

The *Sanctus, Benedictus,* and *Agnus Dei* are movements equal in all respects to their preceding numbers. Nothing in music could exceed the striking originality of the *Sanctus,* while for a true musical inspiration the student may well turn to the 130 bars of beautiful harmonies and melody which constitute the *Benedictus.* The expressive *Agnus Dei* is full of pathos and religious sentiment. The imploring tones to the Lamb of God for ' mercy,' and reiterated appeals for the grant of peace were surely never more tenderly and religiously expressed through the medium of music.

The Mass in C (No. 6) appeared with the year 1816. Compared with so gigantic a work as its predecessor, the D minor, it is a small Mass, containing no more than sixty-five pages or so of MS.; nevertheless, it is written for four voices with full orchestra, and includes an Offertory, a *Laudate Dominum,* and an *O Salutaris.*

The shortness of this Mass in C and others of a similar character is to be accounted for in this wise. The services at the King's Chapel (for which Cherubini by virtue of his office as Superintendent had to furnish the music) were not remarkable for their length, and rather than protract the devotions of the Court Cherubini had to limit the whole of a Mass to the space which he personally would have preferred to allot to one movement. Nevertheless, the brevity of these works is more than atoned for by the remarkable truly soul-stirring beauty of their music.

The *Kyrie* of the C [1] Mass is a chaste movement, more noteworthy for the purity of the vocal writing, and the clever blending of the voices, than for any great orchestral effects or startling harmonies. It ends peacefully enough, and leads to a *Gloria* wherein the same sentiment and colouring are hardly dispelled. The music moves leisurely on, there is no lashing of huge tone-waves, no heaving of mighty forces of wind and string, Cherubini seems resting from his Herculean efforts in the D minor Mass. There is, however, a suggestion of pent-up strength in the opening bars of the fine *Credo*. The deliberate scale passage (*Allegro maestoso*) in G major (the key of the movement), followed by the voices on the words *Patrem Omnipotentem*, is bold to a degree, and gives a swing and freedom to the music which are maintained up to the exquisite *Incarnatus* movement, which latter is led off slowly by first and second *soprani* and *alti* in a beautiful passage of three-part voice writing. The *Crucifixus* is subdued and solemn in character—indeed, it is so shrouded that the bright and triumphant tones

---

[1] The third Mass composed by Cherubini in this key.

of the " *Et Resurrexit* " are welcome theologically and
musically. The close of the *Credo* is original and very
striking, the intermingled *soli* and chorus on the word
" Amen " being skilful and effective in the extreme.

The *Sanctus, O Salutaris,* and *Agnus Dei*—worthy
parts of this beautiful Mass—are thoroughly characteristic of their composer, being clear in outline,
pure in harmony, fresh and life-giving in melodic
vigour and fancy. Some authorities think most
highly of this work. Mr. Bellasis, in his " Memorials
of Cherubini," says that " Cherubini never wrote anything more thoroughly spontaneous." Girod, the
French critic, speaking of this work, says he was
aware of musicians who preferred it to any other of
Cherubini's Masses.

Still there are other grand Masses from the fertile
pen of this musician. The one known as No. 7 in
the key of E flat for full orchestra and voices, was
composed by Cherubini in the year 1816. It served its
purpose in the King's Chapel, till it was replaced in
1818 by the Mass in E (No. 8) for four voices with
full orchestral accompaniment. In 1819 the Mass in
G (No. 9) appeared. This was composed for the
crowning of Louis XVIII. As a concise work, for the
beauty of its music, for the general treatment of its
several parts, this First " Coronation " Mass would
alone be sufficient to win for its composer an
enduring fame as a master in this form of composition. The lengths of the several movements in this
Mass are as follows:—*Kyrie* 101 bars; *Gloria* 503
bars; *Credo* 435 bars; *Sanctus* 105 bars; and *Agnus
Dei* 61 bars.

The B flat Mass (No. 10) [1] came with the year 1821, and four years afterwards the prolific genius brought forward the magnificent work which he composed when Charles X. became King of France in 1825. This is one of the best of Cherubini's works, abounding as it does in points of interest both to the musician and amateur.

" Mass in A, Coronation (No. 11), for three parts," is the description of this latter work as given in the catalogue of Cherubini's writings.

All authorities justly place it high in the list of sacred compositions. Thus Girod in his Treatise *De la Musique Religieuse* terms it, " the most beautiful of Cherubini's Masses." The Kyrie he describes as simple and touching, well characterized, full of loving and confiding sentiments. " The *Credo*," continues the same authority, " is a creation so original that it would be futile to search elsewhere for any resemblance to it." Berlioz, too, speaks of this Mass in the highest terms of praise. Inviting special attention to its Communion March, he says :—" It is a mystical expression in all its purity, contemplation, and Catholic ecstasy. . . . This piece breathes only of Divine Love, of faith without doubt, of calm, of the serenity of a soul in the presence of its Creator; no earthly sound comes to mar its heavenly quiet, and it brings tears to the eyes of those who listen to it. . . . If ever the word " sublime " has had a true and just application, it is *a propos* of Cherubini's " Communion March."

It was first performed in the Cathedral at Rheims

[1] Composed for the King's Chapel; for four voices in chorus and full score.

upon the auspicious occasion of the Coronation of Charles X.

Cherubini wrote other Church music. Passing over the many Hymns, Antiphons, Motets, Litanies, and detached service pieces too numerous to enumerate here, there came two scores, without some reference to which this and any memoir of this classic musician would be singularly incomplete. These are his Requiems.

The one in C minor was composed in the year 1816. The Anniversary of King Louis XVIth's death was required to be celebrated, and this Requiem was composed for this purpose. It was first performed in the Abbey Church of St. Denis on the 21st January, 1817.

It stands musically among the finest compositions of its class. Grand and stately in outline, it yet contains a wealth of detail, and a richness of natural musical scholarship and original power. No capable critic could listen to a performance of this work in its entirety without becoming fully impressed with its magnificence. Its appropriate colouring, the solemn grandeur of its movements, the religious fervour which pervades the whole, combine to make a great and lasting impression on the mind imbued with musical sympathy.

"The Requiem in C minor," remarks Berlioz, is on the whole the greatest work of its author. No other production of this grand master can bear any comparison with it for abundance of idea, fulness of form, and sustained sublimity of style. The *Agnus Dei* in *decrescendo* surpasses everything that has ever been written of the kind. The workmanship of this portion, too, has an inestimable value, the vocal style is sharp and clear, the instrumentation coloured and powerful, yet ever worthy of its object." Altogether this work stands a striking example of sacred exposition combined with consummate contrapuntal knowledge and skill, while it shows also how thoroughly its composer had studied and become imbued with the style of Palestrina, adapting it in felicitous manner to his own individual musical thought and expression.

Most modern Mass music which the great masters of the art have given birth to belongs to one grand epoch in the history of the Mass form. This is the imaginative and dramatic era, and to this Cherubini's Requiems undoubtedly also belong. In the D minor *Requiem* notably has Cherubini become imbued with dramatic fervour, and this at places is so developed that the devotional element appears to some minds to be lacking.

A predominating character in these Requiems— indeed, in all Cherubini's Masses, however—is the strong touch and colouring of Cherubini's pure and noble style; and this pervading element conduces to a sense of complete satisfaction and sacredness of purpose whenever the devotional mind has the accessory aid of such soul-permeating harmony as the master musician now under notice has bequeathed to his Church.

With this work Cherubini made peace with the Royalists at the return of the Bourbons.

Cherubini's second *Requiem* (in D minor) [1] may,

Composed for three men's voices—two tenors and bass. Original MS. consisted of 88 pages full score.

perhaps, be fitly described as his last great score—a
worthy crowning point of a long life—for its composer
was close on fourscore when he finished the work.
According to the catalogue of Cherubini's works it
was composed between February and September,
1836, so that its composer was seventy-six years old
when he began it, and at its completion had just
entered upon his seventy-seventh year. Remembering
this fact, the composition becomes at once a notable
instance of sustained musical capacity, since it is
doubtful whether its composer's great power and
genius were ever seen to better advantage than in
this magnificent composition. Strangely enough this
Requiem was not performed in its entirety until some
two years afterwards.

The *Dies Iræ* number was first given at a concert
at the *Conservatoire* on 19th March, 1837. The work
was first heard in its entirety on the 25th March,
1838, since which time it has been more than once
given at Roman Catholic services in this country.

"It is impossible," writes Mr. Bellasis in his
"Memorials of Cherubini," "to hear or study this
almost unapproachable composition without feeling
how intimately impressed the author must have been
with the whole spirit of prayerful, earnest, mournful
supplication implied in the idea of the Christian
Sacrifice for the Dead." And this is no doubt true.
If Cherubini ever wrote inspiring music, if he ever
soared into the very heaven of Art, it is in the music
of this *Requiem*. Elsewhere he has been masterly,
grand, and learned, but, in no previous work, not even
in the D minor Mass or the C minor *Requiem*, has he

risen from the earthly and poured forth sublimer music—more inspired than created—than is to be met with in this last *Requiem*. For appropriate sentiment, effectiveness in its harmonic combinations, for conciseness, conception, and masterly treatment Cherubini's D minor *Requiem* stands unsurpassed by any similar work.[1]

To do justice to the score in detail would be out of place in the small compass of the present biographical sketch. Yet the student is reminded that it would afford him or her a profitable study to analyze thoroughly this perfect piece of musical craftsmanship ; to note each beautiful phrase, to instance the many ravishing melodies, the successions of grand chords, and cleverly disposed discords, and then to feast in the admiration of those mighty *crescendo* effects and striking contrasts of the tone art, of which Cherubini in this *Requiem* especially has proved himself so completely the master. Every student would do well to acquaint himself with this work, so as to become familiarized with the beauties of a score which ranks among the grandest of sacred musical compositions.

There is not a movement in this famous composition which is not especially noteworthy for its treatment, and which might not be cited in illustration of the masterly musical conception and declaration on the part of its illustrious author. Versed in the traditions of his creed, the first sounds that are heard in this sublime composition are tones which it has been well

---

[1] Mendelssohn greatly admired this Requiem Mass, and in 1838 recommended it to the notice of the Committee of the Lower Rhine Musical Festival for performance thereat.

said "have breathed a prayer of rest for the departed ever since the day when the first Gregorian Mass for the dead was sung." These occur on the word "Requiem"; but that the reader and student may the better realize the devotional spirit of this *Introitus* movement a direct acquaintance with the score must be urged.

The second movement, the *Graduale*, sung after the Epistle, and with voices unaccompanied, is sweet and placid—music like the streaks of gold which break the heavenly cloudland.

All this is in striking contrast to the terrific opening of the *Dies Iræ*, which follows—a movement so wondrous, so stupendous and sublime in its grandeur as to deeply impress the mind whenever it is rendered.

Taken as a whole, this *Dies Iræ* number has rarely, if ever, been equalled in the domain of sacred art. The opening passage leading up to the crash of voices as they give the words *Dies iræ* in the fourth bar is a point of matchless art achievement. Not less remarkable is the strength and solidity of the unisons on the words *Tuba mirum*, with the brilliant outburst upon the A major chord and the flight of the upper voice to the top A. With thrilling effect, too, is the passage *Rex tremendæ majestatis* treated, until it loses its gigantic energy in the soft and placid music, sung *mezza voce* to the words *Recordare Jesu*. The *Lacrimosa dies illa* is a soul-stirring, slow movement leading on to a subdued ending to the word *Amen*.

The *Offertorium* is remarkable alike for its varied and vigorous character and its beautiful harmony.

The Fugal idea at the words *Quam olim Abrahæ*, brief as it is, emphasizes the slow beauty of the *Hostias et preces tibi* music, which in its turn is varied by a thrilling *Allegro Vivo* passage, which brings the movement to a glorious termination. The remaining movements, the *Sanctus*, *Pie Jesu* and *Agnus Dei*, are replete with the most beautiful and appropriate music. In the *Sanctus* a prodigious effect is gained in the treatment of the word " Hosanna."

The *Pie Jesu* number is an excellent illustration of Cherubini's pure grace and contrapuntal ingenuity in quietest mood, and comes in welcome contrast to the mighty tonal outbursts in the *Sanctus*. The *Agnus Dei* opens boldly in the D minor key, but soon its master composer rises with magnificent force, and the whole vocal and instrumental strength is requisitioned at the point *Lux Æterna*—so effective, so awe-inspiring, as to almost unnerve the listener. Then there is calm. Slower and sweeter become the strains, until finally all dies away. All seems to have drifted upwards to realms of restful bliss.

Some writers assert that " the absence of female voices in this Mass was a concession to the Church dignitaries of the Restoration, who, influenced by the bigotry of former periods, wished to exclude female voices from all Church music." Cherubini was hardly the man, however, to be approached, or to apply himself, after such a fashion. A devoted and faithful son of his Church, nothing in the shape of a " concession " would have been asked or expected of him. The planning of the D minor *Requiem* for male voices only was a deliberate art plan. The composer himself, doubtless, sensible of the mould and character of men's voices, as well as of the nature which such a work should partake, preferred the darker colourings obtainable in matured male voices. Designed as the D minor *Requiem* was with some view to his own funeral, Cherubini was moved probably to give it as sombre and grave a tone as possible. It must be allowed that it is pitched throughout in a singularly suggestive and mournful key.

Much as has been said already of the works of Cherubini, only his principal writings have been touched upon. His vast musical thought and activity, his great prolificness—one of the surest signs of genius—is seen in the full length catalogue of his works. In all, there are more than four hundred and thirty compositions, including 23 Operas, 11 Masses, 11 Cantatas, 10 Sonatas, 7 Motets, 2 Requiems, 20 Antiphons, 36 Hymns, 3 Psalms, 1 Oratorio, 1 Symphony, 48 Romanzas; between 60 and 70 detached Airs, 15 Nocturnes, 14 detached Kyries, 6 Instrumental Quartets, 4 Litanies, 4 Rondos, 3 detached Sanctus, 4 Odes, 11 Marches, a Quintet for Instruments, 11 Dances, 14 Choruses, 14 Duets, 9 Terzettos, 7 Pas Redoublés, 5 Canons, 5 Opera finales, 4 sets of Solfeggi, 4 Recitatives, 2 Madrigals, 2 detached Agnus Dei, 1 Overture, 1 Pianoforte Fantasia, a Course of Composition, 1 set of Canzonets, 2 detached Credos, a Sextet for voices, and a host of smaller pieces for the church, stage, and concert room.

DEATH AND RETROSPECT.

On one of the endmost days of November, 1830, the
aged master, Cherubini, stood at the grave of his
beloved *confrère* Catel, but the memory of his *Adieu,
mon bien aimé Catel !* had scarcely faded ere the old
man was bidden to pay the final tribute of affection at
the grave of yet another equally dear to him. In
1834 Boieldieu died, and, cold as was the morning,
Cherubini roused himself early to see the last of a
favourite pupil, one whom he loved well, and with
whom he had worked long. "Gentlemen," said Cherubini at the grave, "it is not long ago since we accompanied here the remains of our fellow-worker, Catel ;
to-day we have to mourn the premature death of our
very dear friend Boieldieu." That such partings
should remind him of his own advanced years is certain. "I shall write a Requiem for myself to which
there will be no objection," he is reported to have
said, upon the authorities refusing the performance of
his "C minor" at Boieldieu's funeral. But the hale
Cherubini clung tenaciously to his duties at the *Conservatoire.* The loss of his colleagues gradually passed
over amid the wear and tear of every-day life among
the *Conservatoire* scholars, and the veteran musician,
now in his old days, loved by many and respected by
all, seemed to grow young again. This, however, was
but a transient state. In 1841 there came the shock

of the death of his son-in-law. The blow was too
heavy a one for the old man. Cherubini never re-
covered himself. With the beginning of 1842 Cherubini resigned his post as Director of the *Conservatoire*,
sensible, perhaps, that his end was not far off. This
proved to be the case. Early in March increased
weakness set in ; he became confined to his room, and
saw none save his family and most intimate friends.
Finally he took to his bed, where he remained until
he passed away at the bid of Death on the 15th March,
1842. He reached the good old age of eighty-two.
His obsequies were held at the Church of St. Roch,
when was performed his Requiem for three men's
voices, a work he wrote after the ecclesiastical authorities had prohibited (because it contained female
voice parts) the performance of the Requiem he
composed for the funeral of Boieldieu. Over three
thousand mourners and friends attended the funeral.
Student and Professor of the *Conservatoire* joined in
the procession, which was made up of persons of all
ranks. To his own music—the solemn strains of a
Funeral March which he had lovingly composed upon
the occasion of the obsequies of General Hoche—all
that was mortal of Cherubini was conveyed to its
long resting-place in the cemetery of Père la Chaise.

Cherubini's death was instantly felt. All France
rose to do him honour at the last. She gave him an
imposing funeral; all her great sons wrote of him ;
streets were named after him ; his name, his virtues,
abilities, and talent were cut in marble; his own
countrymen and the Florentines erected monuments
to him—in short, everything was done to perpetuate

the memory of a great son of art who had won the good wishes of every citizen, and who commanded the admiration of every musical mind.

The daily round of the life of this eminent man was marked by much that must have proved depressing and disappointing to his artist mind. From the outset he had a hard struggle, and it was not until he was verging upon sixty years of age, that honour, position, or income came in his path. During all his young life his pecuniary condition was anything but satisfactory, and he had before him the task not only of earning a livelihood, but of remedying what he conceived to be abuses in art; while beyond all were the larger reforms, especially in Opera, which filled his mind.

The position was one with conflicting features. He might soon have improved his exchequer had he been minded to drag his art down to the level which was required to make him a popular composer. Had he pandered to the *vox populi* and perhaps the publishers, he could probably have dived down deep into their pockets; while, had he lived in such favoured times as now, a few "pot-boilers," such as divinely gifted composers do not disdain to write, would have spared him every care or thought about serious art.

All this, however, was incompatible with the temper of the man, and with that mission which he felt to be his—a mission which he ultimately accomplished.

Thus he went on for many years, hampered and harassed in his musical schemes with petty financial troubles, which a generous hand might easily have alleviated.

While yet a comparatively poor and unsuccessful man, Cherubini, notwithstanding his pecuniary disadvantages, took to himself his wife, and this step we may conclude could scarcely have improved matters.

In 1795, when he was in his thirty-fifth year, the *Conservatoire de Musique* was founded, and Cherubini was appointed one of three Inspectors of Tuition. He perforce accepted the post, albeit it was not one to his liking. He had reason for discontentment. He had laboured long and worthily for the betterment of French music, and no one capable of judging doubted either his claims or capacity for a more responsible and remunerative appointment. His reputation and the love he had for his profession entitled him to higher recognition.

A formidable figure, however, had long stood in Cherubini's path, none other than Napoleon. The great Consul disliked Cherubini, and showed it, and the great musician took no pains to diminish the aversion. In his career of conquest which was to make despotism universal throughout Europe, Buonaparte had effected the crushing defeat at Austerlitz, and though this and similar expeditions kept Cherubini employed in the construction of war music, it banished all hopes of his settling at Vienna, where a congenial sphere appeared to be opening out for him. How preferable this latter would have been to the work of organizing and conducting Napoleon's *soirées* at Schönbrunn—from which no good could accrue either to art or artist—may be imagined.

What was the cause of this dislike between soldier

and musician is not very clear. Possibly Napoleon had not forgotten Cherubini's settings of the Republican songs of the stormy days which preceded the Consulate and Empire, or Napoleon may have been moved by purely artistic motives, for, as we shall see, he was one day gracious enough to indicate to Cherubini the kind of music that pleased and exactly suited his taste.

One honour Napoleon did bestow upon Cherubini— he made him Chevalier of the *Légion d'Honneur*. This was during the Hundred Days.

The abdication of Buonaparte, the restoration of the Bourbons in the person of Louis XVIII., brought sunshine along the path of the long-neglected musician. Almost at once did riches and honour and advancement become his portion. Recognition came from all quarters. The King smiled upon him, he was elected a member of the *Institut*, and now the post of Musician and Superintendent of the King's chapel looked like falling to his lot, for Martini, its previous occupant, had died.

As a fact the post was speedily offered to Cherubini, but eventually he shared it jointly with Lesueur, who had held it with Martini under the former *régime*.

A creditable story is connected with this incident, and as it affords an instance of exceptional consideration, as between artist and artist, I submit it for the consideration of contemporary professors, without much fear that it will be too often emulated, for, in music as the profession is nowadays, there are few men as generously. minded as Cherubini proved himself to be, and given these, it still becomes necessary to find colleagues worthy to be treated as he treated Lesueur. In 1816 the King's first gentleman-in-waiting inquired for Cherubini, and submitted to him the King's pleasure as to the post. "Monseigneur," said Cherubini in reply, "Monsieur Lesueur, my friend, is more worthy than I am of this high position. If I had not a young family to bring up, if I were rich, I should refuse it altogether; but if his Majesty is willing to allow me to share with Lesueur the superintendence of his music, I will accept it with thankfulness." The King consenting to this arrangement, Cherubini shared the office with Lesueur at a salary for himself of 3000 francs per annum.

Further honours were yet in store for him. The Philharmonic Society of London, which had only recently been formed, came forward and offered Cherubini the sum of £200 for a Symphony, an Overture, and a composition for the voice. This was in 1815. It need hardly be said that Cherubini fulfilled the contract to every one's satisfaction. The Symphony in D and Overture in G were performed on the 1st of May and the 3rd of April respectively, and have ever since been regarded as exceptionally attractive musical productions by the *habitués* of these concerts.

In 1822 he was promoted to the Directorship of the Paris *Conservatoire*. His duties in this capacity were such as he delighted in, and he threw his whole energies into the work of raising the standard of the teaching given.

For years and years—indeed, until within a short time of his death—he remained at this post; alternating his useful and conscientious labours in instructing and guiding others with some composition on his own account. Thus was brought to light some of the interesting items which embellish the latter portion of the lengthy catalogue of works from the pen of this truly great and justly esteemed master of musical art.

THE INFLUENCE OF CHERUBINI UPON MUSIC.

DRAMATIC MUSIC.

IN estimating the influence of Cherubini, upon French art or music in general, one very important point needs to be touched upon ; namely, the precise dates between which the composer's career extends. Except with close readers a rambling uncertainty prevails as to the exact whereabouts in musical chronology of this talented son of art. When his name is mentioned the minds of many people wander back to the Scarlatti and Stradella epoch, and not a few enemies to literal dates are bold enough to tack the great contrapuntist's life close on to that musical age when Palestrina was swaying his severe and noble order of art. Not so. Old *habitués* and amateurs can almost touch hands with Cherubini, since he died only nine years before the year of the Great Exhibition in 1851, or two years after the wedding of our present gracious Queen. Let the mind, then, become impressed with the fact that Cherubini is comparatively a modern man, far removed from the dark musical ages to which the careless and superficial enthusiast, unintentionally doubtless, too often relegates the man and his works.

There exist, at least, three distinct standpoints from which the student and reader may endeavour to gauge any influence of this master. These would involve the consideration of his influence upon Opera; a contemplation of his labours in the field of Sacred musical art; and finally, some thoughts concerning the effect he exercised as a Teacher and moulder of the musical tendencies of those who had the advantage of his personal tuition.

It is upon the French School of Music that we should expect to find the influence of Cherubini most perceptible, for though an Italian by birth and musical education, he became closely identified with French art, rather than that of his own country. Writers, too, always—though unnecessarily—associate him with the French school.

In Cherubini's day there was not a little art *matériel* in France upon which to set his impress. A hundred years before his eyes first met the blue Florentine sky, Opera had had its rise in the French capital, under the auspices of Cardinal Mazarin. Cambert, a Parisian organist, had produced the first French opera, *La Pastorale,* and then came Lully, erst kitchen scullion, who rose to be chief musician to Louis XIV. Lully did away with some of the everlasting airs and duets of the imported Italian style of opera, and in their place extended the chorus, introduced the *ballet,* and originated the overture. Rameau appeared with further improvements by way of greater variety, both of harmony and melody in the vocal and band parts, besides instituting that now world-famed art species, the comic opera or *opera-bouffe.* Grétry followed, and

gave a decided French character to the national music.
He readily caught and turned to account all the
subtle points of expression and humour in his *libretti*,
while his piquant and original melody, together with
a continued expansion of the orchestra, led to much of
the *verve* and elasticity which has characterized French
opera ever since. The development of comic opera
was far more marked than grand opera, and while one
seemed to hit the popular taste, the other awaited the
advent of musicians of the stamp of Cherubini, Halévy,
Meyerbeer, and Berlioz, men with the capacity to
peesent this art feature with all that richness of
ensemble and surrounding without which it might
have appealed to the French people in vain. As it is
serious opera has taken no great hold upon the
French people. Meyerbeer is the chief composer
beyond Cherubini who has identified himself with *opera
seria*, and his unparalleled success was due in a large
measure to gorgeous externals. Other modern men,
Flotow, Offenbach, Lecocq, all, save Gounod, have
laboured in the light and frivolous vein of *opera-bouffe*,
or something closely akin to it.

Another composer who has left his mark upon the
dramatic music of France was Piccini. He was
writing operas before Cherubini was born, and, settling
in Paris in 1776, he gave himself up to the task of
re-establishing Italian opera upon the old lines, as
opposed to the new ideas and reforms which Gluck
(1714-1787) was promulgating. These reforms of
Gluck's tended towards a general simplicity, an avoid-
ance of difficulties tending to indistinctness, greater
subserviency of the music to the poetry, and the ex-

tinction of much in the way of melodic redundancy, together with other abuses attaching to Italian opera of the day.

Thus, dramatic music was no unknown art quantity in France when Cherubini appeared as Gluck the Second, a champion of fresh reforms ere the air was well cleared of the smoke from the famous Gluck and Piccini "war." It was Gluck's work which Cherubini felt impelled to carry on. He was a born purist; his training under strict and legitimate mastership accentuated this; and throughout his long career he departed not from the lofty and noble walk of art which he chose out for himself. According to Gluck, "the mission of music was not merely to afford gratification to the senses," but to become the vehicle of expression of the moral qualities. With this Cherubini quite coincided; and although the French people heard the exposition of the dogma, time has proved that France has really been unimpressionable to the teachings of both Gluck and Cherubini.

The national taste in France was decidedly towards flimsy comic opera, as it has been ever since; and, previous to Cherubini, grand opera in its true sense had received little attention from composers. This was owing partly to the national temperament, partly to the fickleness of public taste, and not a little of the preference for a light style of Opera might be traced to political causes. War was in the air. Ever and anon men and women were restless with political excitement. Serious plays and still more thoughtful cadences were ill adapted to such an age and national temper. Cherubini saw the situation, and, despite all

obstacles, determined to give effect to his convic-
tions as to a reasonable and an elevated musical
drama. *Démophon* was prepared, and this was his
initial step in the work of founding a grand style
of French opera. Old Italian habit, force and tradi-
tion, all were forsaken for a style of purer and
sterner mould. *Lodoïska*, more advanced in the
new fashion, followed, and with its unusual harmonic
combinations and instrumental effects, both startling
and brilliant, staggered public and musicians alike.
Both works had novel features in the improved treatment of the choruses, in the form of the concerted
pieces, and in the concise arrangement of the finales
and principal movements; while compassing all was a
surrounding of noble expression hitherto unknown in
French stage music. In *Medée*, that powerful imagination which belonged to Cherubini more than to
French stage composers before him, is even more
decidedly expressed. This opera, as is known, abounds
with music of the most passionate character, always
subjugated by that pure, classic idealism which
tempered its composer's musical vein. Yet, as if to
dare on the score of versatility, in a subsequent opera,
Les Deux Journées, he effected an entire change of
front. In this great score, which is something of a
connecting link between *opera seria* and *opera comique*,
is presented a domestic story of thrilling interest.
The composer is both at the height of his dramatic
powers and the fulness of idyllic realization. The
work reveals itself as a chapter out of real life, and all
is painted in a simple, unadorned—if pictures are
way. Nowhere has Cherubini been extent preses-

seldom has he presented a more joyous picture than in
the *Deux Journées*. It has been called the "masterpiece of comic opera," so enjoyable is its music, while
a great critic says of it, "The situations are as serious,
and the incidents are as interesting as any story of
domestic interest ever set; and the choral writing and
the orchestral colouring are as vivid and graphic as
any to be found in Mozart and Meyerbeer." All this
the French people had placed before them. What
was and has been the result?

Of the reception in their day of these principal
among the operatic works of Cherubini we have already
read. What has been their bearing upon French
dramatic art since?

It must be allowed that the influence of Cherubini
upon French Opera has thus far been but temporary.
In his capacity as Chief of the *Conservatoire* he
imbued many notable students there with his views
and aims, and some of this teaching necessarily
reflected itself in the styles of the eminent among
such scholars. But one and all supplanted their
mentor in the estimation of the French public. He
took no lasting hold on the hearts of the French people,
and it is only for historians to confess that it was in
Germany that Cherubini's works found the most
enduring appreciation in their composer's lifetime and
since.

To look beyond French dramatic music for any sign
of his art sway is equally unnecessary. If he remained
unimitated in France it is unlikely that his style and
cadences would be appreciably adopted in Italy or
temper. Cherubini given over as it was to melodic

indulgence to excess; the latter already in possession
of a national dramatic art, having much in common
with the Cherubini style, and only needing the romantic
touches of a Weber to place it absolutely beyond the
pale of the impressionable from without.

As a fact, Cherubini has exercised no durable
bearing upon the lyrical music of either France, Germany, or Italy, any more than he has affected the
dramatic music of the English lyric stage. He was,
however, both understood and highly esteemed in
Germany, not only by the people at large, but by
individual masters of the art. Beethoven regarded him
as the greatest opera composer then living, and when,
in 1805, Cherubini arrived in Vienna to fulfil an en-
gagement to write an opera, the two masters not only
became close friends, but the great symphonist
allowed his vocal music to be largely influenced by
Cherubini's style, and, what is more, was not ashamed
to own it. To this day Cherubini is more to Germany
than to France. Under the title of the *Wasserträger*
the *Deux Journées* is well known upon German opera
boards, while in Vienna this same opera and *Medée*
are often performed to the delight of the thoroughly
musical public of that city.

As an opera composer, then, let it be finally admitted that Cherubini made no permanent impression
upon the French lyric stage. Writers affirm that he
created Méhul, Lesueur, Spontini, Halévy, etc., which
to an extent is true, but it would be both inaccurate
and misleading to say that he founded a school, or that
in Cherubini could be recognized one whose works and
style had been copied to any great extent by res-

succeeding composer. Doubtless his operas found many admirers—even Haydn and Beethoven were such— but they rarely served as models for lesser French composers, who for the most part were bent upon hitting the popular taste of their day with a form of art less stately in form and bereft of much of that pure idealism which stood a stumbling-block between the lofty-minded composer of *Medée* and a too ecstatic public.

In Germany Cherubini, although he did not influence the national art, made some temporary fame as a successful essayist in reformed dramatic art. The gigantic lyric creations of Mozart already existed : albeit it has been declared that had there been no *Deux Journées* the *Fidelio* would never have been written, Beethoven being inspired not less by Cherubini than was the latter by Mozart. If, therefore, the beautiful and classical score of *Les Deux Journées* prompted *Fidelio* only, the world of music has much for which to thank Cherubini. Happily there is more. Many maintain that in this masterpiece—the *Deux Journées*—Cherubini created the late Wagnerian theories of operatic treatment, since there is no *aria d'entrata* for *prima donna*, tenor, baritone, or bass; while no solos interrupt the action of the drama. " Every character is individualized, and has a marked type, each one contributing to the concerted pieces faithfully, consistently, and coherently." It is incontrovertible, moreover, that in this opera Cherubini struck the first blow in the system for annihilating the tyranny of leading singers in operas—quite an accepted Wagnerian tempɾv.

Mention has been made of the leading features of Cherubini's operas. It only remains to say that most of them were written for the French lyric stage. In his principal operas he sought out a new path. He discovered his road in *Démophon*, and he confirmed this in *Lodoïska* and his later operas. His improved operatic style partook chiefly of greater variety in harmonic combinations, novel and original instrumental effects, a regard for concise and agreable proportion in the movements, a jealous control of melodic extent and propriety—indeed, such a general remodelling of accepted style and method as made his operas quite unique in the order of French lyric music. It is not surprising that to Gaul and Italian they failed to serve as models. Of a mixed mould, Cherubini's operas belong not to the French nor to the Italian school; indeed, as regards this latter their composer deviates to the utmost from the accepted Italian style of his day. So far as Cherubini's influence goes, little of this accrues at present from his dramatic music. The final judgment upon it has yet to be made. It is by no means improbable that when the suspended verdict is given upon such soundly constituted art work it will be the unqualified approval of a later posterity at such lofty and idealistic art as flowed from so pure and fresh a source.

Church Music.

As a composer of Church music the name of Cherubini stands out in striking relief. Throughout music's growth sacred art has been at once both the greatest aspect and noblest medium of musical expression. The mind needs only to dwell for a while upon the vast number of rich and glorious scores of a religious vein—and, if possible, to imagine the world without all such reverent art—to arrive at an adequate estimate of its worth either as an aid and stimulant to devotion, or as music *per se.*

In the slow but sure process by which the present age has become enriched by this precious bequest of sacred art, many notable names, from St. Ambrose to the Church musicians of to-day, come down to us. Chief among these stand those great tone poets— Mozart, Haydn, Beethoven—who all contributed largely to the Mass music of the Catholic Church. In his Masses Cherubini places himself upon an equality with these masters of the art, so that, while adding fresh jewels to an already rich treasury, he is enabled also to assert a just claim of place among the first rank of sacred musical writers.

The very qualities which barred the way to his acceptance as a successful dramatic composer were well calculated to aid Cherubini towards a great reputation in the field of sacred composition. His pure idealism and lofty tone and character; his profound learning and the constant expression he would give thereto; his chaste and classic melodic tendency; his thoroughly controlled passion and periods of powerful imagination —these were characteristics, natural or acquired, much more suited to the church than to the stage. Gifted as he was with the power of-exciting emotion, he bridled this force in no unhesitating way, so that rarely in any of his works are to be found such periods of tremendous feeling and pathos as surround the character of

Medée, in the powerful opera of that name. In his Church music he is serious, some say to dryness. His power of restraining his emotional capacity here stands him in great good stead. Remembering, too, his rich gift of melody, one he refused to give way to even in secular music, there is in these sacred works a remarkable absence of all but the most legitimate musical material as a means to the end desired. Thus the consensus of opinion seems to favour the sacred rather than the secular music of Cherubini as the most valuable and characteristic portion of his art work. Before extending some remarks upon Cherubini's sacred music—already touched upon in the earlier portion of this monograph—let us take a glance at Church musical art as it existed prior to Cherubini's contributions thereto.

Church music had had many a devotee, many a pious exponent before Cherubini aided its cause. In his own land there had lived, laboured, and died the grand procession of ancient classical composers, from Josquin des Prés, past Festa, Palestrina, Monteverde, and Carissimi, on to the pure school of Durante, Pergolesi, Leo, and more. No pupil had been better trained in the traditions of this old Italian church music style than was Cherubini; few students applied themselves with greater assiduity to the absorption of its overpowering properties than did he.

But this was not the species of sacred musical art which obtained in Italy in Cherubini's day. The sway of composers and people was towards an indulgence in melodic excess of the worst kind. Operatic flight, fancy, and rhythm—these barely sufficed to satisfy the craving of the intoxicated *signori* and *lazaroni* alike for seductive and rapturous tune. Every organist and chapel-master was drawn into the stream, and priests and vocalists went with them. To construct church music to suit a taste of this kind was attended with no difficulty, and piles of so-called sacred music, surcharged with an abundance of theatrical melody, filled the service books, etc. Little of such has survived to indicate its tone and character, which is not to be wondered at nor to be deplored. In Rossini's *Stabat Mater*, first performed in 1842, the genius and taste of the age in the matter of religious music reached its culminating point, and it only needs the labours of a devout worshipper, Roman or Protestant, to examine the several numbers of this avowedly sacred composition, to arrive at an approximate idea of the ebb to which Ecclesiastical music had sunk in Italy.

In Germany Church music had long been triumphant, and Chorales, Motets, and Passion music— much of it tempered with the quaint severity of the old Netherlands school—were in existence to give tone and colouring to the Masses of Bach, and later on to those of Haydn and Mozart. The glorious contribution to sacred musical art, which the Haydn and Mozart Masses constitute, had been completed long before Cherubini devoted himself to religious music, but it is improbable that he was influenced in any way by its existence. As a student he probably knew little of such Masses, nor would they perhaps have been an open book to him at any time, unless they were contained in the library of the *Conservatoire*.

His notions, then, concerning Church music may be accepted as exclusively his own.

Cherubini's Church music stands a great rebuke to the array of church musicians of Italy, as well as of France, who from the middle of the Eighteenth century seem to have become lost to all remembrance of the lofty grandeur and nobility of style bequeathed them by Carissimi, Palestrina, Scarlatti, Leo, Durante, and Jomelli. Trained in Italy, Cherubini witnessed the latest art tendencies. He could see music, whether for church or stage, drifting into a channel of mere melodic display. In the former in particular, masses, requiems, motets, and occasional pieces for the most solemn moments in the service were made vehicles for the display of tunes and rhythms barely creditable as canal songs or ditties for the *osterie*.

No doubt whatever exists as to the reality of Cherubini's services to music for the Church. His elevated temperament, his love of purity in art, his great mastery over contrapuntal form and device, his sympathy with the old Italian church composers, all qualified him for the task of composing music which should not only ennoble and remodel a degraded taste, but also supplant an unworthy art-form in the highest service in which it is possible for music to be employed. But, given his example, and his value as a model—the importance of which to the cause of art evangelization generally cannot be too highly estimated—there yet remains the question—did he, or did he not, found a school of sacred music for France or any other country? The answer must be made in the negative. Acquainted as he was with the works of the old Italian church com-

G

posers, imbued as he also was with a high sense o
the dignity and purity of style which music for the
altar should possess, this led him no farther than to
the composition of sacred music, which will serve for
all time and ages as samples of what Church music
should be in colour, sentiment, and construction. Low
as was the ebb of Church music throughout the
dioceses of France during this composer's lifetime, still
worse as it was and has since remained to this day in
Italy, no band of young composers flocked to the new
standard, so that to-day Cherubini stands. little more
than the noblest and purest Italian musical model
which the Roman Church has possessed since the age of
Palestrina and of Allegri before him. The Roman
Church, like the Anglican, is not advancing musically,
and few new scores, meritorious or otherwise, help
to swell the lists of Mass and Motet to which the
great sons of art have contributed so liberally.
It is to be regretted that this question of supply
will not apply to the Anglican Church. In this
case much new music is hourly composed and published, but little of it deserves the name of sacred
music when placed beside the compositions of Croft,
Purcell, and Wesley. When, however, a new son of
art does arise to embellish the Roman Church service
with fit music, let him follow in the footsteps of
Cherubini rather than those of Rossini. Emulating
the pure grace and chaste style of the former, such a
one will then add an ennobling and not a debasing
element to the cause of Religion; he will be making
a worthy offering to his Church—an offering which,
alas! can only be too rare in this age, given over as

it is to unctuous harmonic combination and a still more seductive melodic exuberance—this whether in music for church or stage.

As a Teacher.

As a Teacher, Cherubini exercised much immediate bearing. In the case of the pre-eminently great musicians, they for the most part lived and worked amid the surroundings of their homes and lodgings. Now and then a digressive spirit like Schubert found not a few of his noblest inspirations amid the freer air of the *bier-garten*. One and all, however, were indirect preceptors, who taught the world through their works rather than by word of mouth, and students of the art profit by their teachings just in so far as they possess and exercise the patience and the intelligence to fathom the mighty scores of a Mozart or Beethoven; thus to become acquainted with the great musical truths which such works contain.

Cherubini was otherwise. He was a direct teacher, and in his days many a scholar—the dull one and the brilliant—had the advantage of his personal advice and guidance. As Teacher, Examiner, and finally Director of the Paris *Conservatoire* many students came under his notice, and remembering the great theorist's love for his art, his earnest purpose, and sound musical teaching, it becomes impossible to estimate too highly either the extent or value of his instruction.

If pupils like Auber, Halévy, Carafa, Zimmerman, Batton, and others whose names might well be perpetuated, caught something of his healthy vein, then the unseen sway of the master may really be more than it will ever be possible accurately to gauge. Thus much for those who came under his influence during his lifetime.

There remains, however, that wider world of learners to whom he spoke, and continues to speak, in direct personal language. All theorists of music since his day are under obligation to him, and there is probably no student of Harmony and Composition, who has not met, and become indebted to, the valuable Treatise on " Counterpoint and Fugue " which Cherubini published in 1835, and which has more than once been translated into English. It proves its author to have been a perfect master of technical detail, and Cherubini would have served the *Conservatoire* well had he bequeathed it nothing more than this work and the other numerous exercises he wrote for the benefit of its scholars.

This work still remains a standard text book, and has, no doubt, served as a model for every similar course or treatise upon the same subject published since.

It is as a great exemplar in musical art that Cherubini may best be regarded. He stands at once a model reformer and teacher, one who had discovered for himself the doctrine of purity and depth in art, and was determined to promulgate his views. It was no new teaching, for the fathers of the ancient Italian Church style had passed away impregnated with it; nor was it a theory having for its effect the undermining of the foundations of true art. Cherubini was no heresiarch. Rather than pull down the structure of music he would prop it up with all the support of weighty foundation, in the shape of material upon which a so grand and ever-increasing edifice could rest. Surface matter, triviality in melodic skip and unctuous progression, superficiality in place of depth and learning, these were ominous indications to him of a diseased art tendency. To stem this, so far as he could, became his mission; and the sight of the great man, lost to personal ambition and aim, battling against the elements which jeopardized his art is no ignoble one. He was no melody-monger, nor throughout his works can he be traced pandering to the popular clamour for tune. His polyphonic writing is always consistent and remarkably grand. The sound early training he received from Sarti stood him in good stead throughout all his long after career. Unless it be Mendelssohn, no composer has surpassed Cherubini in his broad and grand style. His muse, deliberately a severe one, is always clear and well-defined. His vast theoretical capacity never escapes notice, and he worthily ranks with those masters of counterpoint who have combined great genius with a profound study of contrapuntal art. Like Bach, Handel, Mozart, and other notable contrapuntists, however, his scores frequently exhibit instances of how even the severest laws of counterpoint may be broken, and this with beneficial, often very happy, result. With all his learning, Cherubini is always perfectly understandable, and if his music cannot by all be regarded as consistently enjoyable, it can be asserted of it that it never fails to arrest the attention of even the careless listener; while to the true musician and man of understanding and culture it commands imme-

diate admiration, and is at once a source of pleasure
to the ear, and an intellectual treat to the mind.
Throughout all his works his sense of music's real end
and purpose is apparent. Gluck was the founder and
teacher of the religion of dramatic truth. Then followed Beethoven and Cherubini—great apostles of
Gluck—the former, in his *Fidelio*, accentuating the
new teaching; and Cherubini, notably in his operas,
carrying the doctrine into far wider-reaching terri-
tories. Depth of feeling, earnestness of thought and
purpose—in fact all inner emotion find expression in
Beethoven and Cherubini in a much more marked
style than as enunciated by Gluck or Mozart. It
does not lessen the value of such model teaching and
example because so little of it has been adopted. It
exists in example for all time. In Cherubini's day Italian
dramatic music promised to develop into little more
than an exuberant melodic overgrowth. The deeper
and secret veins of musical expression were promising
to become lost, and probably would have been, save
for the noble creations that emanated from the master
musicians just enumerated—composers who have given
to the world scores which must ever remain unassail-
able and unsurpassable, because they are composed
of the indestructible elements of musical scholarship,
and earnest emotional truth and expression.

We shall do well to forget Cherubini as one who
affected the music of his own, or the present, day to
any appreciable extent; not thinking of him either as
the founder of any school. Another generation may
look back upon a resuscitation of his works, sacred and
secular, and profit by his magnificent services to art.

This experience belongs not to us. We tack too
closely upon his life and surroundings to judge of his
ultimate bearing upon music. We do know, however,
that he had few, if any, followers to carry on his work,
and therefore, whatever bearing upon future art is to
be his, must depend upon the persistency with which
present-day students apply themselves to his scores
and adopt the sound art principles upon which he
worked. He stands the great philosopher of modern
musical art. Contrasted with all other composers he
occupies quite a unique position. He travelled a long
way towards being on a level with Mozart, Beethoven,
and Mendelssohn, but he cannot seriously be ranked
with these great tone poets. His power seems to be
of most magnitude when we look upon him as a great
example and model : then his influencing force is
always more objective than reflective. He is something of a beacon—warning musical workers of all
times from the rocks and shoals of the tawdry and
trivial in art. More good, it might be maintained,
has been, and perhaps will be, done by his example
than has been accomplished by his scores. The result
should be none the less sure, for though unwilling
scholars may hesitate to emulate him in depth of
study and profundity of learning—which the present-
day music publisher does not care for—Cherubini is
always with us as a permanent ideal for all who
aim at purity in art combined with all dignity and
originality.

Much has been said and written concerning the
lasting properties of Cherubini's muse, and not a few
point the finger of scorn to the measure of appreciation

extended nowadays to it. It must be admitted that Cherubini's music is not altogether in fashion—at any rate in England—and that in concert programmes of every kind it is rare to find items from the pen of this classic musician. But much the same fate has attended other great masters of the art, and many instances could be cited where a composer and his works have been neglected for years and years after his lifetime—only to be one day resuscitated to the delight of an enlightened age, and to the end of the permanent endorsement of a deserving name on the scroll of enduring fame. For the season there is no great demand for Cherubini's music. His operas are rarely given, and little of his instrumental music is heard. Consequently, beyond his Overtures, and the performance of one of his Masses occasionally, Cherubini is an unknown quantity to the rising generation of musicians. It is not improbable, however, that a reaction may set in at no distant season in favour of Cherubini, and that his scores, sacred and secular, may be as sought after as they are now neglected. It must not be forgotten that his writings are based upon the sure foundation of sound art principle, and strictly legitimate musical aim and purport. He has left many—very many—scores which can well preserve his fame ; but it would be difficult in this day to predict with safety as to whether his dramatic or sacred music will find most favour with a generation to come. Much of this result must depend upon the turn which social, political, and religious events may take after our lifetimes. Undeniably his principal Operas, his important Masses,

the Overtures, and a few minor pieces deserve the
title of great and masterly music, and the world's
repértoire of finest music would remain singularly
incomplete without such compositions. The Masses
and Requiems especially go far to place Cherubini in
the front rank of musical master minds. It is to be
regretted that the extreme length of the best of these
precludes their frequent performance in churches ;
but so it is at Roman Catholic as well as Protestant churches nowadays—the disposition to devote
much time to devotional matters is becoming marked
by a grudging rather than generous spirit, consequently opportunities for hearing such sublime Church
music—under suitable conditions—are becoming more
and more rare.

All summed up, then, the influence of Cherubini,
either through his sacred or secular music, is singularly
undetermined. It cannot be denied that the world of
music—composers, performers, and listeners—all admire his high and lofty vein of style; and when
his noble music is listened to, all become impressed and
delighted with its ideal beauty and noble sentiment.
Here matters end. They do not retire to their closets
and imitate him in melodic turn and harmonic combination after the same fashion that hosts of workers
have imitated Mendelssohn. What lump of creative art
talent in any country has Cherubini leavened ? No !
his works and style lack qualities which find imitators,
of which by the way there are always enough when
there is a fruitful field for the imitative capacity.
Did his scores possess the immediate properties which
have brought the music of many other great composers

into every home and every heart, a readier popularity would have awaited Cherubini in his own day. As it is, much that is grand, beautiful, and unimpressionable (only because it lies so low from the surface) in Cherubini's music will remain, perhaps for an age, the portion only of the inquiring and thoughtful musician. The art of the universe will become but slowly permeated by its influence; but it is not too much to predict that truth, as Cherubini has written it, will in the end prevail, and that the sound principles upon which he worked, and the high ideal which was his, will ultimately meet with the approval of those minds most cultivated. Music has its evolutionary processes, and recognition of nobility in art must come even though it be long delayed. Cherubini rests for a season, the great preacher of purity in art, rather than an impressionist; but already he will not have lived and worked in vain, if students emulate his classic idealism, his beautiful part writing, his masterly contrapuntal facility, his chaste melodic interpretation, his complete freedom from mannerism, his broad and masterly stroke, and above all his marked devotion and allegiance to art. A really great man, musically and morally, Cherubini stands out in bold relief amid a mass of musical contemporaries, and whatever may be the verdict of posterity regarding his influence upon art, no doubt can ever exist as to the calibre of his writings, which most emphatically stamp their originator as a truly great musician—one who just missed the highest reaches of highest art.

TEMPERAMENT AND DISPOSITION.

In his temperament Cherubini was what school-
girls term a Philistine. Doubtless he was a good
husband and parent, but unfortunately for himself,
and sometimes for others, he belonged to that class of
men who can never get on with the world. He possessed an irritable and sensitive nature, he was cross-
grained and crotchety, and while other people
would appear to be gliding along smoothly and
contentedly, Cherubini was everywhere meeting with
friction. He lacked that rare quality—tact, and he
seems to have been unaware of any solatium with
which to charm away the petty annoyances of every-
day life.

In some respects he deserves indulgence. Notwithstanding that he had done an immense amount of
work—for Cherubini was a great worker—he remained
very poor, only receiving regular emolument as a
salaried professor at the *Conservatoire.* His operas had
not been sufficiently successful to enrich their author,
and a musical reputation only is not pre-eminent as a
trusty prop when one is forced to mix constantly in
the highest circles of any society, to say nothing of
that then at Paris. Crœsus and Midas need to come
by and lend a helping hand to the struggling genius
bent on reform, or the dissemination of any new
doctrine. He was evidently not born under a lucky

star. Thus, when just making great headway in
Vienna—whither the composer had gone in 1805,
sick at heart with the state of affairs in Paris—it was
unfortunate for him to encounter the man who of all
others could thwart his purposes. Napoleon had
marched to Vienna after his victory at Austerlitz, and,
finding Cherubini there, ordered some music. " Since
you are here, M. Cherubini, we will indulge in some
music." Thus was Cherubini forced to provide several
concerts at Schönbrunn, where was the summer palace
of the Emperor of Austria. And all this without
reward such as other musicians of the French Court
received!

Many men would have been guarded in face of so
evident a disadvantage. Not so Cherubini. He
elected to fall out with one whom it is only fair to
admit could vie with him as a son of Mars if not as
a devotee of Apollo, although Napoleon was really no
bad judge of war music. " Your music is so noisy and
complicated," said the First Consul one day to Cherubini, " that I can make nothing of it." The reply
was tantamount to, " Excuse me if I don't think it
necessary to adapt my compositions to your brains! "
and the reader will probably agree that if Napoleon
had been a clown, instead of the first man in Europe,
Cherubini could not have snubbed him more.

On another occasion the great general told Cherubini to his face that his music was too learned and
too German, that in preference to it he liked the
strains of Paisiello and Zingarelli, for which criticism
Cherubini continued sullen and ungracious towards
the Consul. Napoleon, in fact, took every opportunity

to blunt the enthusiasm and efforts of Cherubini. The students of the *Conservatoire* once bore part of some obloquy. Napoleon having returned victorious from the Second Campaign, the students begged the General to grant them permission to perform a Festival Cantata and a *Marche Funèbre* by the master. The soldier overlooked the request!

As is so often the case with men tempered and constituted as was Cherubini, his own experience did not leave him more considerate towards others, and it is not libelling him to say that those who happened to be under his control, say at the *Conservatoire*, seldom had a good word for him. The only exception probably was in the case of any promising and highly talented pupil, such as Halévy, or Adam, or Boieldieu. " He was only rough outwardly," we are told, but it is unfortunate for his reputation that his worst points, his uneven temper, his irritable manner, his brusqueness, independence, obstinacy, his critical severity, his satire, reserve, and general dissatisfaction were the first qualities to show themselves, and which had first to be surmounted ere any ordinary mortal could hope to gain the good grace and interest of the presiding genius.

"The independence of character," says a great critic, " which Cherubini possessed, rendered him a subject of terror to all who came in contact with him; the musician who had taunted Napoleon in smart repartee was not likely to be very conciliatory to inferiorities and mediocrities." As a set-off to this, there is the testimony of a writer in the *Harmonicon*—a defunct periodical, far superior in its literary-musical contents and critical acumen to any publication of the present day—wherein it is stated that "Cherubini had the happy art of gaining over the singers to his views by a suavity of manner and a conciliatory mode of address not always possessed by one of his talent and profession." This, however, was as early in his career as 1789, when he was Director of the Comte de Provence's *troupe* of Bouffons, and before he had become soured by some of his mundane experiences.

To tell all the stories concerning Cherubini's strange character would be out of place here; but it is impossible to forget Mendelssohn's description of the unpolished man as "a burnt-out volcano, all covered with stones and ashes;" or Berlioz's amusing story of an eruption of this Vesuvius.

Cherubini had assumed the Directorship of the Paris *Conservatoire* in 1822. The proverbial new broom did its work, and many supposed abuses, tolerated under the rule of his predecessor Perne, were disputed, and disposed of accordingly.

Among other things it was forbidden to students of both sexes to enter the school by the same door. Berlioz (who entered the *Conservatoire* four years later than Cherubini) also bore a terrible character for turbulency, and determined that he would set the above regulations at nought. Going one morning to the library, and pretending ignorance of this rule, he (Berlioz) entered by the door in the Rue Bergère, assigned to the lady pupils. He had scarcely reached the library door before he was stopped by a servant, who told him to go out and return to the same spot by another entrance. This was ridiculous, and

Berlioz refused to comply. The *serviteur* made his way to Cherubini's room, and acquainted him with the matter. Berlioz meanwhile had secured a score of Gluck's "*Alceste*," and was absorbed in it, little dreaming that any further notice would be taken of his innovation. Cherubini entered the library looking more cadaverous than usual. "After passing several students at the table," says Berlioz, "the servant lighted before me, and cried '*Le Voilà!*' On recognizing me, Cherubini snorted with rage. 'It's you, is it? *C'est vous qui entrez par la porte, que'—que'—que' ze' ne veux, pas qu'on passe!*' he continued with his comical Italian accent.

" 'Sir,' I replied, 'I did not know of your order; another time I will take care to conform to it!'

" ' *Une autre fois! une autre fois! Que'—que'—que' venez-vous faire ici?*'

" 'You see my reason for being here,' replied Berlioz, as he pointed to the volume before him, 'I come here to study Gluck's scores, and I have no need of any one's permission to do that. The library is public from ten till three. I have a right to make use of it.

" 'Th—th—the right?'

" 'Yes!'

" 'You shall not come here again. *Comment vous appelez-vous?*' cried Cherubini, trembling with rage, and I in my turn answered, 'You shan't know it!'

" ' *Arrête, a—a—arrête le, Hottin!*' shouted Cherubini; '*que'—que' ze' le' fasse zeter en prison!*' whereupon the two gave chase round the table without succeeding in catching me. I put an end to the scene by taking flight, shouting as I went that the intolerable Cherubini should neither have me nor my name, and that I would soon return to study the scores."

Again, in the case of Beethoven the composer of *Medée* was not slow to complain of that very characteristic which was so strikingly marked by its absence in himself. ' *Il était toujours brusque*,' was his invariable comment and reflection upon the character and disposition of Beethoven. Cherubini, however, allowed no impression of this kind to prejudice his unbounded admiration for the compositions of this king among orchestral composers.

The name of Cherubini is surrounded with a fund of anecdote—some of it complimentary and creditable, not a little the reverse. How much of it is true it is hard to decide. All that can be said is that many of the stories concerning him have been *on dits* in their day, and are as true as *on dits* in general. With this provision the reader may be tempted to linger over a few such, characteristic as they are of the man, and furnishing as they do a glimpse of his natural disposition. Some of them fully bear out the reputation which Cherubini has gained for being a sour, cross-grained old gentleman. Others are the direct opposite in drift and character, and point to quite a genial and considerate disposition on the part of the great theorist. How gratefully Spohr writes of the reception which Cherubini accorded to him and his compositions! Here are the words of the composer of the *Die Wiehe der Töne* symphony :—

" From the frequent opportunities I had of playing before Cherubini at private parties, I conceived a very

ardent desire to have all my quartets and quintets, so
far as I thought them worthy of it, heard by that by
me highly esteemed master, and to introduce them by
degrees to his notice, in order to ask his opinion of
them. But in this I succeeded with very few only,
for when Cherubini had heard the first quartet (it was
Nr. 1 of the Op. 45 written at Frankfort), and I was
on the point of producing a second, he protested
against it, and said: 'Your music, and indeed the
form and style of this kind of music, is yet so foreign
to me, that I cannot find myself immediately at home
with it, nor follow it properly; I would therefore
much prefer that you repeated the quartet you have
just played!' I was very much astonished at this
remark, and did not understand it until I afterwards
ascertained that Cherubini was quite unacquainted
with the German masterpieces of this kind of Mozart
and Beethoven, and at the utmost had once heard a
quartet by Haydn at Baillot's soirées. As the other
persons present coincided with Cherubini's wish, I
consented the more readily, as in the first execution
of it some things had not gone altogether well. He
now spoke very favourably of my composition, praised
its form, its thematic working out, the rich change
in the harmonies, and particularly the fugato in the
last subject. But as there were still many things
not quite clear to him in the music, he begged me
to repeat it a second time, when we should next
meet.

"I hoped he would think nothing more about it, and
therefore at the next music party brought forward
another quartet. Before I could begin, however,

H

Cherubini renewed his request, and I was therefore obliged to play the same quartet a third time.

"The same thing occurred also with Nr. 2 of Op. 45, excepting that he spoke of it with more decisive praise, and said of the adagio : ' It is the finest I ever heard.' He was equally pleased with my pianoforte quintet with the concerted accompaniment of wind instruments, and I was frequently obliged to play it on that account."

That he could be just and generous towards a brother artist—not always an easy matter—is seen in the following :—

A pedant once went to Cherubini complaining of a flagrant fault in the novel chromatic progression from F sharp to F natural in the well-known *Dal tuo Stellato* in Rossini's *Mosè in Egitto*. Thus :—

* Thus :—

" What do you say to such a libertine's act ? " inquired the pedant.

" What do I say to it ! " exclaimed Cherubini; " why, I am only sorry I was not its perpetrator."

Like all truly great men, too, Cherubini could see merit in his compeers. A joyous student once came to him full of a certain performance of one of Beethoven's symphonies. Cherubini rejoined, " Young man, let your sympathies be first turned to the creative, and be less anxious about the executive in art;

accept the interpretation and ponder over the creation
of those wonderful compositions, which are written for
all time (and for the imitation and criticism of all
nations."

It was Cherubini's judgment and encouragement
which led the father of Felix Mendelssohn Bartholdy to
decide upon music as a profession for the youth, who,
not long afterwards, surprised the world with that
wonderful example of juvenile capacity, the Overture to " The Midsummer Night's Dream." In 1825,
Mendelssohn being 16, the father took the boy to
Paris to consult Cherubini. Under the lad's arm was
the B minor Quartet for strings. Cherubini said,
" Le garçon est riche, il fera bien, il fait même déjà
bien."

Cherubini possessed a wonderful aptitude for saying
smart things. Sometimes there was sting in them,
at others they were harmless enough.

One day he was confronted by one of those bores
of humanity who are incapable of directing their own
rudder of life, and who constantly want the advice of
other people as to the best course they should take.
It was a certain French singer with a tremendous
voice, but who could not decide the line of art for
which he was best fitted. Cherubini begged him to
sing. Vocalist opened his mouth, and the foundations
well-nigh trembled with the bellowing.

" What shall I become ? " said Furioso when he had
finished.

" An auctioneer," replied Cherubini.

Upon another occasion a friend presented himself
before the master with a score said to be Méhul's.

After examining it, Cherubini remarked, "It is not Méhul's, it's too bad to be his."

"Will you believe me, M. Cherubini, if I tell you it is mine?" said the visitor.

"No! It is too good to be yours!"

An instance of his frank criticism was provided when Beethoven's *Fidelio* was first performed at the Karnth-nertor Theatre, Vienna. Cherubini was present. At the conclusion of the performance he was asked how he liked the Overture, the "Leonora in C." "Well," said he, "to be honest, I must confess that I could not tell what key it was in from beginning to end."

That such criticism was prompted by no base motives may be gathered when we remember the estimate he put upon the genius and work of the composer of the "Choral" Symphony. He accounted himself as nothing to a Beethoven. At a certain concert he once found in his hand a programme in which was inserted, sandwich-like, one of his own overtures—that to *L'Hôtellerie Portugaise*—between two compositions by Beethoven. Noticing the dangerous proximity, Cherubini remarked to a friend, "Look here, and see what they have done. I'm going to appear a very small boy."

He was strongly opposed to ill-deserved success— as he had reason to be, seeing how favours and honours had been showered upon less deserving musicians than himself at the French Court—while he long remained with little more than a bare subsistence. "*Malheureux!* are you not ashamed of such un-deserved success?" In such terms did Cherubini

accost Boieldieu after one of the performances of the
Calife de Bagdad at the Feydeau Théâtre; which
brusque admonition Boieldieu took so much to heart,
that he did not attempt another opera for three years,
during which period he received the advantage of
training from Cherubini, and then produced *Ma Tante
Aurore* with extraordinary success.

It was Cherubini who has furnished us with one of
the best solutions yet propounded to that serious
problem for thoughtful minds—how to keep one's
·umbrella. One day he was walking along a *boulevard*
when it began to rain. A gentleman, recognizing the
maestro, pulled up his horse, and begged that
Cherubini would take the reins and drive home
quickly out of the rain. He could not accompany
him, as he was going in a contrary direction, but he
proposed borrowing the composer's umbrella.

"No, I never lend my umbrella," was the abrupt
reply, and, whatever we may think of the courtesy,
there can be no doubt about the prudence of the
musician.

Cherubini was generally esteemed a great talker,
but withal he could make good use of the golden
quality of silence, especially if the topic under consideration was not commending itself to him.

His favourite pupil, Halévy, one day invited the
master to the theatre to hear a new opera which
Halévy had composed. At the end of the first act its
composer asked Cherubini how he liked it. No reply.
With the second act completed, the question was
again put. No reply. Halévy warmed. "*Vous
ne me répondez point*," he exclaimed. Still no

reply. Halévy jumped up exasperated, and left the box!

Professor John Ella, in his charming "Musical Sketches," tells the following of Cherubini :—

This learned *maestro*, more renowned for his wit than for his sensibility, on meeting Tulou, the flautist, returning from the funeral of the oboe-player, Brod, was thus addressed :—

"Ah! *maestro*, we have lost our dear friend Brod."

Cherubini, who was deaf, exclaimed, "What! what !! what !!!! "

Tulou repeated with a loud voice, "Brod is dead ! "

"Ah!" said the stoic Cherubini, turning away, " *Petit son, petit son !* " (little tone).

It is to be feared that the master was more intent at the moment upon differing with Tulou himself, for although Brod's tone was not loud, his taste and intelligence placed him in the highest rank of executants, and Cherubini must have been sensible of this. The flute was never a favourite instrument with the great theorist, and one day he was even heard to exclaim in disgust, "The only thing worse than one flute is two."

Ella vouches, too, for the following incident, which goes to prove that Cherubini could at times exercise that demonstrative kindness characteristic of his countrymen :—

Having composed an Offertorium for a grand public religious festival, Cherubini was informed on the eve of its performance of the sudden illness of the principal tenor vocalist. Early next morning the invalid's part was sent to young Begrez, with a request that he would study the music, and sing it before noon at the place appointed. In vain did violinist and amateur vocalist plead inability, Cherubini was peremptory, and assured the *debûtant* that he had the greatest confidence in his musical intelligence. At the performance the admirable singing of Begrez produced a deep impression, and at the end of the service the illustrious Cherubini rushed to the front of the choir, and cordially embraced him in the presence of the whole congregation. After this Begrez placed his violin aside, took to singing, and became a successful vocalist.

Not always did Cherubini have matters his own way. His residence in Paris covered one of those stormy times which at different periods have swept over the fair capital. In the revolutionary days of 1792 the quiet and peaceably-disposed citizen hesitated to venture in the streets by day or night. Cherubini hazarded the risky and perilous experiment, with the result that he had perforce to submit to become the principal figure in a practical illustration of the saying, " A fiddler in spite of himself ! "

Once, writes Mr. Bellasis in his " Memorials of Cherubini " : —

" During an occasion of more than ordinary excitement, Cherubini fell into the hands of a band of *sans-culottes* who were roving about the city seeking musicians to conduct their chants. To them it was a special satisfaction to compel the talent that had formerly delighted royalty and nobility to minister now to their own gratification. On Cherubini firmly refusing to lead them, a low murmur ran through the crowd, and the fatal words 'The Royalist! the Royalist!' resounded on all sides.

"At this critical juncture, one of Cherubini's friends, a kidnapped musician too, seeing his imminent danger, thrust a violin into his unwilling hands, and succeeded in persuading him to lead the mob. The whole day these two musicians accompanied the hoarse and overpowering yells of that revolutionary assemblage, and when at last a halt was made in a public square, where a banquet took place, Cherubini and his friend had to mount some empty barrels, and play till the feasting was over." This was in 1794.

As a man and a musician one turns from the consideration of Cherubini's life with regret, for there is a wholesome atmosphere of honesty about his purpose and career which is no less refreshing than are the pure and lofty strains of music which streamed so bountifully from their chaste source. Music such as Cherubini's must always be cherished by the student because of the purity of the element of which it is composed, and it can always be resorted to when, with senses jaded with harmonic luxuriance and sickly melodic sentiment, the better nature is struggling for some healthier region of artistic experience and realization.

CATALOGUE OF CHERUBINI'S WORKS.

VOCAL COMPOSITIONS.

COMPOSITION.	DESCRIPTION.	COMPOSED.
CANTATAS : 11 in all.		
1.	*La Pubblica Felicità* ...	... 1774
2.	*Amphion*	... 1786
3.	*Circe*	... 1789
4.	*Clytemnestre* ...	... 1794
5.	*Pour la Goguette*	... 1812
6.	Louis XVIII. *Fête* ...	... 1814
7.	City of Paris *Fête* ...	... 1814
8.	*Inno alla Primavera*	... 1815
9.	Royal Guard Banquet	... 1816
10.	*Le Mariage de Solomon*	... 1816
11.	*Hôtel de Ville Fête* ...	1821
CREDOS : Detached.		
1.	Credo, for eight voices and organ ...	1806
2.	Credo, in D, 4 parts	1816
MADRIGALS.		
1.	*Ninfa Crudele*, five voices ...	... 1783
2.	four ,, ...	... 1811
MASSES : 11 in all.		
1.	Mass, in D, four voices	1773
2.	Mass, in C ,, ,,	1774
3.	Mass, in C ,, ,,	1775
4.	Mass, in F, three ,,	1808

COMPOSITION.	DESCRIPTION.	COMPOSED.
5.	Mass, in D minor, four voices	... 1811
6.	Mass, in C, four voices ...	... 1816
7.	Mass, in E♭ ,, ,, ...	... 1816
8.	Mass, in E ,, ,, ...	... 1818
9.	Mass, in G ,, ,, ...	... 1819
10.	Mass, in B♭ ,, ,,	... 1821
11.	Mass, in A, three ,,	... 1825

MASSES, REQUIEM.

1.	C minor, four voices ...	1816
2.	D minor, three ,, ...	1836

MOTETS : 7 in all.

1.	Motet, four voices	1777
2.	Motet, with solo for Marchesi	1781
3.	Motet, *Nemo Gaudeat* ...	... 1781
4.	Motet, Septuagesima Sunday	... 1818
5.	Motet, *Lætare Jerusalem* ...	... 1823
6.	Motet, *Sciant Gentes* ...	... 1829

ODES : 4.

1.	18th Fructidor (Poignards)	... 1797
2–3.	*Anacréon* Odes...	... 1799
4.	Emperor Napoleon's Marriage ...	... 1810

OPERAS : 25 in all.

1.	*Il Quinto Fabio*, No. 1	1780
2.	*Armida*	... 1782
3.	*Adriano in Siria* ...	... 1782
4.	*Il Messenzio*	... 1782
5.	*Il Quinto Fabio*, No. 2	... 1783
6.	*Lo Sposo di Tre Marito di Nessuna*	... 1783
7.	*L'Idalide*	... 1784
8.	*L'Alessandro Nell'Indie*	... 1784
9.	*La Finta Principessa*... ...	... 1785
10.	*Il Giulio Sabino*	1786
11.	*Ifigenia in Aulide* ...	... 1788
12.	*Démophon*	... 1788
13.	*Lodoïska* ...	... 1791
14.	*Kourkourgi*	... 1793

COMPOSITION.	DESCRIPTION.	COMPOSED.
15.	*Elisa*	1794
16.	*Médée*	1797
17.	*L'Hôtellerie Portugaise*	1798
18.	*La Punition*	1799
19.	*Les Deux Journées*	1800
20	*Anacréon*	1803
21.	*Faniska...*	1806
22.	*Pimmalione*	1809
23.	*Le Crescendo*	1810
24.	*Les Abencérages*	1813
25.	*Ali Baba*	1833

PSALMS, 3, including—

1.	*Dixit*, four voices	1774
2.	*Dixit*, Solo and Chorus	1775

The above are the principal vocal works. In addition, Cherubini composed at different times a large number of lesser vocal compositions, notably the following :—

Agnus Dei, 2.
Airs (Detached Pieces), 62.
Album Pieces, 2.
Antiphons, 20.
Ariettas, 3.

Chansonette	1834
Canons, 1 set, two, three, four voices ; 5 detached	1807

Duets, 14.

Introits	1824

Kyries, 14.

Lamentations, 2, two voices...	1776
Litanies, 4, four voices	1779

Latin Words, Settings of, four voices.
Latin Hymns, various.

Magnificat, four voices	1775
Oratorio (without title)	1777
Pasticcio, " Epicure "	1800
„ *La Prisonnière*	1799

| COMPOSITION. | DESCRIPTION. | COMPOSED. |

Quartets, 2.
Republican Hymns and Choruses.
Romances.
Sanctuses 3.
Solfeggi, 4 sets (160 in all).
Sextet, 1.
Te Deum, four voices ... 1777
Terzettos, 9.
War Songs, 2.

INSTRUMENTAL COMPOSITIONS.

MARCHES : 11 in all, including—

1.	March	(Night Patrol) ...	1806
2.	March	(General Hoche)...	1797
3.	March	(Republican) ...	1800
4.	March	(Baron Braun) ...	1805
5.	March	(Wind Instruments)	1808
6.	March	(Wind Instruments)	1809
7.	March	(Wind Instruments)	1810
8.	March	(National Guard)...	1814
9.	March	(Funèbre)... ...	... 1820
10.	March	(*Faniska*)...	... 1831

MINUET, Full Score 1808
NOCTURNES : 6, for Piano 1782
OVERTURE, 1, in G, Full Orchestra... ... 1815
QUARTETS : 6 in all.

1.	Quartet, in E♭	1814
2.	Quartet, in C	1829
3.	Quartet, in D minor ...	... 1834
4.	Quartet, in E	... 1835
5.	Quartet, in F	... 1835
6.	Quartet, in A minor ...	1837

QUINTET, in E minor 1837
SONATAS : 10 in all.

1.	Cylinder Organ ...	1805
2.	Cor Anglais and Piano	1804

SYMPHONY, Full Score ... 1815

Among the lesser Orchestral works are the following :—

COMPOSITION.	DESCRIPTION.	COMPOSED.
Ballet Music	*"Achille à Scyros"*	... 1804
Bassoon Pieces, 2		... 1818
Canzonet (Piano) ...		... 1782
Chaconne, Full Score		... 1785
Clavichord Sonatas, 6 ...		1780
Clarionet Pieces, 2		1824
Country Dances, 6, Full Score		1808
,, ,, 3 ,, ,, ...		1809
Entr'actes, 2	*Lodoïska*	1805
Figured Bass Pieces (Piano) ...		1798
Hautboy Pieces, 2		1818
Intermezzi, 2.		
Organ Sonata ...		... 1780
Pas Redoubles, 7 ...		... 1814
Pianoforte Capriccio... ...		... 1789
,, Fantasia ...		... 1810
Pieces for Wind Instruments, 8		... 1814
Romances, 18 (Piano) ...		1787
Trios, 2 (Violin and Piano) ...		1793
,, 2, Full Score		... 1810

In all Cherubini composed some 430 Pieces, nearly 100 of which have been published.

NOTE.—For distinguishing many of the above compositions a relative name or incident has here been associated with the scores.

INDEX.

LONDON :
PRINTED BY GILBERT AND RIVINGTON, LIMITED,
ST. JOHN'S HOUSE, CLERKENWELL ROAD.